After she closed the lanai door behind her, she inserted the key into the door. Before she could turn the lock into place, Kevin walked over and took the key from her. "I'll get this."

In the process, his hand brushed against hers. While she wasn't sure those chills should have gone through her skin at his touch, she felt somehow connected to him because of the contact. Katie strolled into Bev's line of vision on the other side of Kevin and gave her an obvious wink. Heat flashed across Bev's face, and she silently warned Katie with pursed lips and a wrinkled brow.

Had Kevin meant to touch her hand, or was the graze accidental? While embarrassed to admit a spark flickered gently within her, she also wondered if she could fan the spark into flame. Suddenly, her hundred reasons for staying away from this man had dwindled to zero.

DONNA L. RICH

has loved books and writing since childhood. She authors contemporary and historical romance and is a member of American Christian Fiction Writers and The Christian Writers Guild. Her successful genealogy research led to her membership in the Mayflower Society. Donna and her husband live in Indiana and adore their beautiful blended family of six married children, seventeen grand-children, and three great-grandchildren. You may find out more about her at www.donnalrich.com.

Books by Donna L. Rich

HEARTSONG PRESENTS

Love for the Right Reasons

Donna L. Rich

Heartsong Presents

So many thanks go out to the Lord for JoAnne Simmons,
who awarded me with my first contract, which was presented to me
at the 2010 American Christian Fiction Writers Conference.
Thank you, Rebecca Germany, for my second and third
Heartsong Presents contracts. Also, a writer is nothing without
the copy edit and the person who does it. Thanks, Wendy.

A note from the Author:

I love to hear from my readers! You may correspond with me by writing:

Donna L. Rich
Author Relations
P.O. Box 9048
Buffalo, NY 14240-9048

ISBN-13: 978-0-373-48648-9

LOVE FOR THE RIGHT REASONS

This edition issued by special arrangement with Barbour Publishing, Inc., 1810 Barbour Drive, Uhrichsville, Ohio, U.S.A.

Scripture taken from the Holy Bible, New International Version®. NIV®. Copyright © 1973, 1978, 1984, 2011 by Biblica, Inc.™ Used by permission. All rights reserved worldwide.

This is a work of fiction. Names, characters, places and incidents are either the product of the author's imagination or are used fictitiously, and any resemblance to actual persons, living or dead, business establishments, events or locales is entirely coincidental.

Chapter 1

The sweet scent of jasmine saturated the air as Bev Lahmeyer took a broom to the front steps of the Lake Serenade Diner. Numerous lacy yellow butterflies moved erratically from one blossom to the next, bringing a sunburst of color to the otherwise dingy appearance on the outside of the restaurant.

They'd had a huge crowd this June morning, more than the ten or fifteen locals who normally gathered, and they were about to get another customer. A late-model green van slowed while two teens doing acrobatics on skateboards coasted in the opposite direction.

Bev headed inside and stuck the broom in a far corner. "Looks like we have more people coming in, Nora." Bev tucked one side of her shoulder-length blond hair behind her ear and watched out the window as the van turned in and parked in the gravel lot. The man got out and walked around to the passenger side to open the door.

"Ooh, the man's not too bad looking. I'd say he's easily in his late fifties."

"Nora." Bev had observed his casual yet impeccable style, but that didn't mean she was interested in anything more than looking.

"Bev, you never know when your Mr. Right may come along."

"You and I've been friends for a long time, Nora, but don't play matchmaker with me. Not many good men come around for a fussy woman in her fifties."

"This is Florida, the land of retirees, and Huff has been gone for a long time. Sooner or later, someone else will come."

"He looks younger than retirement age, but I would imagine he's coming in here to eat, not find a woman. Besides, I want a man who has character, one who believes in God and His ways." *One who can overlook my past and forgive what I can't.*

"So, do you want me to take care of them?"

"The way they're both dressed, they're probably out on a breakfast date. I'll give them white glove service. You go ahead and take that hubby of yours to his doctor's appointment."

Nora untied her apron and headed for the kitchen. "She's a bit overdressed, but I'm just glad for another customer. That restaurant up on the interstate has taken the bulk of our business this past year. Tips have been slim. Have fun!"

Bev hurried to set two paper placemats with fifties memorabilia printed on them on a clean table by the window, placing the paper napkins, silverware, and Coca-Cola glasses in their order on top of the placemat and a coffee cup beside each glass. They'd have the best seats in the house.

The woman walked through the door first, strolled in as far as the cash register, and gave a couple of blinks with well-mascaraed eyelashes. Her flowered red georgette dress with a loosely tied scarf of the same fabric wrapped around her neck gave her an air of sophistication.

He walked in behind her, gave the restaurant a leisurely once-over, and seemed to be in awe over the Coca-Cola, *I Love Lucy*, and *Happy Days* collectibles decorating every nook and cranny. Eventually, his attention shifted to Bev as she walked in their direction. Bev followed his eyes as they ultimately focused on her white tennis shoes and folded-down, ruffled socks.

For a split second, she panicked. Her uniform, a yellow, cotton shirtwaist dress with white buttons running from the pleated, ruffled collar to where her apron was tied around her waist, fell far short of being as glamorous as the red dress on the woman who'd just walked in before him.

It's okay, Bev. This is your job. You have to dress this way. This man isn't any different than any other man who's walked into the restaurant over the last ten years. She gave him her best smile, but the rise of his bushy dark eyebrows and better smile got to her.

Bev brushed the other side of her hair behind her ear and grabbed two menus. She tried to focus on the woman. "Good morning, folks. Isn't it a beautiful day out?"

The woman readjusted the scarf around her neck, setting off a disagreeable aroma of French perfume. "It is wonderful out this morning. We have two of us needing a seat, hon."

"I love your accent. I've been here all my life, and I've never managed to acquire any accent. Would you follow me, please?" Bev took a couple deep breaths before the woman's perfume caught up with her.

"I'm from the Carolinas. That's where my accent comes from. I've been in both states but was born south."

"Florida is unique in that respect," laughed Bev. "We've managed to acquire a blended group of people from all around the world with accents as variable as the stars in the heavens. How about right over here by the window?"

"Thank you, honey." The colorful woman towered at least three inches above Bev's five feet four, but most of her height had to do with her white, open-toed pumps. "I'm looking forward to getting off these feet. Now where is that man?" With a roll of her eyes, the woman looked back to the register, where he sorted through the *Laverne and Shirley* DVDs. "Yoo-hoo, over here."

The man was dressed considerably more casual in a beige, knit polo shirt. He tugged at the tight neck and unbuttoned the top button then pulled the shirttail out of fashion jeans embellished with white embroidered trim on the back pockets. His light-brown canvas shoes were loosely laced with knots at the end of the laces instead of being tied. With a flourish of overzealous fanaticism, he raced to the table and gave Bev a wink. "Thank you, ma'am."

Middle-aged men down here had a tendency to wink at everyone, but that flirtation still gave her a start. The youthful sprout of whiskers on his cheeks, chin, and upper lip suggested he was younger than his gray hair let on. He had a full head of hair except for two slightly receding areas at the top on either side of his high forehead. Hopefully, he didn't notice the flush she felt in her cheeks.

He pulled out a chair for the woman at the same time he raised his brows and nodded to Bev.

Bev fussed with her straight hair. His acknowledgement made her wish she'd spent more time on her hair and makeup today. People always told her she looked ten years younger than she was, but that did nothing for her confidence this morning. As he sat down, a thin smile crossed his lips. Bev handed them the menus. "Are you folks new to Lake Serenade?"

He opened the menu and scanned it from top to bottom, but the woman spoke up first in a thick, southern dialect. "Honey, I travel a lot. Every place is new to me. This gentleman here with me—"

"Hattie, they have your bagels here."

Their body language spoke louder than their words. The woman was taken aback by his interruption, but he had made it clear his business was just that: his business. Bev rattled off her waitress lingo. "Well, welcome to our town. We have a few specials this morning listed on the blue sheet paper-clipped to the menu. Coffee is free with your meal. Can I get you both a cup?"

The woman grasped the tip of her scarf with her thumb and first two fingers, yanked the flurry of color from her neck, and then leaned down to loosen each heel from the backs of her feet. "I will have an espresso, if you have any. This is such a lovely restaurant. Whoever came up with the idea to decorate the diner in this fifties style?"

Espresso? If she wanted espresso, she'd have to travel to the north side of town to Gaston's Coffee Bean and get a cup. Bev slid her fingers behind her starchy collar and lifted the fabric away from her neck. "Tom, the owner, decorated the diner. He and his wife met in the fifties. I guess you might say decorating in the fifties style is his way to bring a bit of nostalgia to Lake Serenade. I once tried to talk him into updating to an espresso machine, but he didn't see the need. I can make you a double-strong cup of coffee, if you want."

Before she answered, the man held his menu out to Bev, smiled, and shook his head. "Only Hattie Lincoln, South Carolina's most unique interior decorator, could arrive in the middle of nowhere and expect a brew of espresso. She'd appreciate you brewing a double-strong cup of coffee. I'll have a cup of regular strength. Thank you."

Hattie glanced at Bev, raised her brows, and forced a laugh. "He thinks I'm a kook."

With a nod in the woman's direction, Bev took the menu from him and left the table. She had the impression she'd stepped inside a few waves of sarcasm rolling between the couple.

She headed for the break room to use the small coffeepot to make the strong cup of coffee. While she measured the coffee into the strainer and a cup of water into the well, she moaned when she caught her image in the mirror in front of her. The starched yellow piece of fabric stuck on the top of her head reminded her of whipped cream on top of a sundae. She'd tried to tell Tom not to expect his waitresses to wear the fabric-covered cardboard that represented a fifties-style waitress's hat. *What is it about the man who just came in that makes me worry about my appearance?* Bev unpinned the fabric and laid it beside the coffeepot.

She set a cup underneath the spout, pushed the start button, and waited for the coffee to brew. Within a few minutes, the dripping had stopped and Bev headed back to the table with the double-strong coffee and set it in front of the woman. "There you go. I hope the coffee's to your liking."

"Thank you. That'll be perfect, honey."

"Have you folks decided?"

He smiled and gave her a nod. "The lady will have a bagel with strawberry cream cheese, if you have any, and I'll have a couple eggs, once over, wheat toast, and a glass of skim milk, please."

"You got it. I'll go place the order, and your food should be out in no time." Bev headed for the kitchen, scribbled out the order for Max, and held the paper in front of his face. "Got an order for two more eggs. Can you do, Max?"

Max stooped down and pulled a skillet from the metal shelves under the griddle, sliced a two-inch piece of butter from the stick that sat on a plate near the griddle, and tapped it off into the skillet. "I saw them come in. I'll fix the eggs in the skillet. The griddle's all ready for lunch. How do they want the eggs?"

She clipped the order to the narrow wire clothesline that stretched across eye level above the griddle. "Over easy. Let me know when the order is ready. I'll be out at the lunch counter working."

"I'll take it out."

"Thanks." Bev grabbed a blue container of salt and headed back out into the restaurant to fill saltshakers. However, the woman's spicy fragrance blended with the stale bouquet of bacon and well-done toast to create a unique mixture of migraine-enhancing aromas. She stilled a quick pang of nausea. Even so, she was desperate to come up with a good reason to open the window and the door even though the heat outside was building up to a ninety-four-degree day.

Oblivious to anyone and anything other than her

pain, she poured salt with one hand and dug her thumb and index finger into the bridge of her nose with her other hand. Soon, Max took the order to the couple's table. She noticed the man signaling her and set the box of salt on the counter and made her way to his table. "Is there something I can get for you?"

The words rolled off his lips like a song. "Do you mind if I open this window? I've recently come down from New York and love to feel the warmth of a gentle summer breeze while I'm enjoying my breakfast."

Bev perked up. "I love an open window. I'll get it."

Who cared that chameleons were likely to crawl into the restaurant with this open invitation? She not only opened the window next to his table but also opened two windows on the opposite side and one window on the forest side to bring in a cross breeze, then stopped briefly at their table. "You folks have everything you ordered?"

Hattie dipped her knife into the container of strawberry cream cheese. "Everything looks delicious. Thanks, hon."

Bev couldn't help but notice his eyes held a silvery blue sorrow. Yet, if she took his whole face into account, his blue eyes were innocently commanding and inviting. Even if she did have an inkling she'd like to know more about where he came from, there were probably a hundred reasons why she shouldn't entertain the idea: He was from the North, he was a vacationer, and she had no desire to get to know someone who preferred cold to sun or would be leaving town soon.

After she'd replaced the last of the lids on the saltshakers, she wiped the outsides clean then shined them with her apron. She vowed to herself she wouldn't allow her attention to wander in his direction anymore. Each time she failed, he returned the glance. He was only being friendly. Besides, playing the little distancing game where she imagined someone was flirting with her was safe. Anyway, she didn't think she was ready to let go of her former husband, who had outshined any man she had ever known. *So, there you have it, Bev. Your life will never change because you live in a fantasy life, and you're afraid to move on.*

Chapter 2

Bev locked the lanai door, set her purse on the floor, and settled down into one of a pair of Victorian wicker rockers. She'd found the high-backed, antique chairs at the flea market, which was a yearly event at the fairgrounds on the north end of the panhandle town. The overstuffed, pale aqua cushions were her creation and matched the ruffled valance decorating the tops of the windows on three sides of the lanai.

The foam cushions folded her into welcomed relief after a long day on her feet at the diner, where the most exciting thing that ever happened was when an occasional handsome visitor showed up. It'd been three weeks since the last one—the visitor from New York—had come.

Her only consistent caller, a cardinal who sat on the bird feeder outside the lanai door warbled his *purdy, purdy, purdy* as he watched over his mate, who was with him. She pecked at the seeds he'd pushed from the feeder to the ground below. Bev had the perfect vantage point.

She closed her eyes, rolled her head to the side, and brushed her hand across the rattan table, its age concealed with her mother's peach linen round, and the white lace overlay draped on top. She could almost feel Huff's presence as sure as she felt the flow of air sweeping through the opened windows from west to east. Arm's length and a hand's stretch across the table was his empty chair.

Tucked into the forest primeval that edged Lake Serenade on one side, the doublewide mobile home was one of forty similar homes anchored in the mobile home park occupied by the over-fifty crowd. Hers was larger than some of her friends' homes and held even more square feet, once Huff had built the lanai addition.

Numerous plants Huff had potted and grown populated the lanai, including the six-foot, unkempt philodendron pompously rising behind her, the luxuriant palm tree nesting in its rattan basket in the front right corner, and three pots of streaming begonias hanging from the ceiling. She rested her hand on his chair, wondering after all these years what it might feel like to have his rough gardener's hand entwined with hers once again.

She and Huff had married right after he graduated from the University of Florida, and they moved into a small apartment in downtown Lake Serenade. They'd saved every penny they could with the hope of buying their own home. Nevertheless, Huff bought a small garden shop with the money they'd stashed away. Eventually, they accumulated enough again to buy the mobile home.

As much as she wanted to linger in her memories, the wonderful respite turned into a revolving door of chaos as her neighbors, Helen and Robert Morgan, called her name in the distance. The distress in their voices volleyed her to her feet.

Four homes away, Robert led the way to Bev's home, with Helen trailing behind. Other neighbors emerged from their homes to see what was going on. Robert stopped on the other side of Bev's car and squinted to see into the lanai. "It's back," said Robert. "Did you see it come up this way?"

She peered out, looked around, and didn't have to guess what *it* was. Many of the homes had been visited by the scaly reptile over the last two weeks. The conservation officer was of the opinion someone had released a pet into the wild, since gators didn't usually have their young until early fall. "That little one?" Living alone, Bev had learned to be brave, but she was not too quick to open the door.

"Little but mighty," said Robert. "He's starting to grow larger. Helen and I sat watching him from the dock. I had thrown out a couple of fishing lines like I normally do around sunset, and next thing we knew, we saw it lying up on the shore. We watched him for a spell, and then I saw him waddling up this way."

"Oh dear. Did you call the conservation officer? You do remember that he wanted to be contacted the next time we saw the gator." Bev knew Robert had his hands full just taking care of his wife, Helen, nearly a stranger now after the Alzheimer's diagnosis.

He pointed to the shed. "No, I didn't, and I hate to tell you, but I kept him in my sight all the way up into your shed over there. Want me to take a look?"

Bev had heard every word, but it didn't register. She

glanced at the gaping hole in her shed that the little gator had visited several times over the past week, and then her eyes zeroed in on an older-than-average golf cart, at least for this complex, putt-putting up the street.

The striking man in a deep-blue polo shirt and jeans captured her attention. He was the man who had come into the restaurant a few weeks earlier. A young woman in yellow, short shorts and a faded, white Pensacola Beach T-shirt sat next to him with her feet propped up on the front bar. Bev's stomach took a little catapult.

He parked the cart to the side of the street a little ways behind where Helen stood and turned off the motor, and then headed into her yard. "We meet again."

"Yes, we do."

"Your neighbor at the bottom of the hill told me a gator came up this way." He motioned to the shed. "Is he in here? I'll get him. I was born and raised down here and used to play with those things, if you can believe that."

Bev tucked her hair behind her ears, glad that she'd stuffed her apron and pixie hat in her work locker. He'd seen her twice now in unsophisticated clothing. "I guess I ought to get the hole taken care of."

A smile, friendlier than the voluminous display of deep-pink azaleas at the side of her neighbor's porch, drew Bev's attention. It belonged to the young woman and grew bigger as she gave a wave to Bev. Bev glanced in her direction and waved back returning the smile.

Seeming to take the stranger's intervention in stride, Robert thrust his palm about five inches from Bev's face. "Stay where you are, Bev. You know how quick this gator is. We'll take care of catching him."

She barely heard him because the stranger melted all her doubt with a smile finer than the smile on the young

woman had who'd come with him. His shirt brought out
the blue in his bashful eyes, which seemed fixed on her.
"Do you have a broom, ma'am? I'll detain the little fellow with the straw end before I clamp my hand around
his jaw. That's all I'll have to do."

She felt a slight amusement at his show of bravery
and suddenly realized she wasn't thinking about Huff
anymore, but rather she was thinking about this man.
As an after-thought, she quickly shook any thoughts of
attraction from her mind. "I'll be right back out." After
she made her way inside her home, she raced past the
laundry room into the kitchen and conducted a frenzied search for the broom. Had her heart revived at this
most inopportune time?

Then she remembered she'd broken a compact of
blush when she dropped it on the ceramic floor in her
bathroom, earlier. Not wanting to keep the man waiting, she rushed through to her bathroom and found the
broom leaning against the wall. She sprinted back out
with the broom, trying to appear as though she had everything well under control. She did, didn't she?

"Here's the broom." Bev looked around for the New
Yorker and guessed he'd gone into the shed, but before
long, the door opened, and the man walked out cradling
the gator like a baby in one arm and clamping its jaw
shut with his opposite hand.

Robert made a feeble motion of his hand to the shed.
"He beat me to it."

Bev gave him a reassuring nudge. "But you're the
one who tracked the gator. We never would have known
he was in there if you hadn't tracked him. Thanks so
much."

The stranger's shaggy brows rose naturally in the
center and synchronized with his smile. Grayish hair

cut in a youthful style and lips forming a big smile, he boasted of his conquest in catching the gator. "Thank you, but I don't need the broom anymore. I already got the little fellow. When he headed back behind a lawn mower, I grabbed his tail and pulled him out."

The familiar sight of stubble growing across his upper lip and along the structure of his jawbone gave him a boyish charm. She felt her face flushed again. Perhaps she should have made a bigger deal of his conquest and tried to win his favor.

She leaned the broom up against the lanai and ran her fingers across the alligator's bony back. "Hmm. I think you'd better think twice about coming up this way again, little one."

He tightened his grip around the struggling reptile. "By the way, my name's Kevin."

She smiled demurely. "And I'm Bev."

"You're not afraid to touch him?"

Bev chuckled. "I've lived here all my life, and I've done more than play with these things. I've dressed them up in doll clothes and put make-up on them."

He narrowed his eyes. "You expect me to believe you?"

"You mean you don't?"

"You're an excellent waitress, but we both know you couldn't have held one of these things still enough to dress them in doll clothes." He winked again as he broke in to her personal space. She subtly backed away, pretending to adjust the broom against the lanai.

The girl traipsed over to Bev and thrust her hand out to greet her. "Hi. I'm Katie Johnson. I'm his granddaughter. Gramps, you know she's telling the truth. Didn't you tell me grandma used to do the same thing when she was still around?"

Bev wondered if he was widowed or divorced or simply didn't wear a wedding ring. How did the lady he was with at the restaurant fit into his life? She cleared her mind of these frivolities and accepted Katie's assertive shake. "Thanks, for the vote of confidence, Katie. I hope to see you around more often. We like for our residents' families to show up for a visit. I'm Bev."

Katie released her hand, and her hasty about-face led Bev to think she didn't like the close proximity of the gator. "Oh, we don't know anyone here," she said. "We've moved here from upper New York. I'm Ticonderoga-born-and-raised, and this is my first trip down this way. I'm staying with my grandpa and mom closer to town. Maybe we can get together sometime."

"Uh, sure." She glanced at Robert, hoping his pride hadn't been wounded when Katie's grandfather had interrupted his valiant quest to catch the gator.

Robert raised his hand in a wave. "See you, Bev. I'm headed back to the lake." He turned to Kevin. "Thank you, sir, for taking care of our friend there. I don't suppose he'll be back this way anytime soon."

Bev focused on Robert and Helen as they ambled down the hill. She took a deep breath and turned her attention back to Katie. "Drop by sometime, or give me your number, and we'll make plans. Or, better yet, I work at Lake Serenade Diner each day, usually from seven till three. Maybe you could stop in. I'll give you a soda on the house."

"You work… ?"

"Time to go." Kevin pointed the gator toward the cart and nodded to Bev as he turned to follow Katie. "Nice meeting you again. We've got to get going."

Bev brushed a few hairs from her forehead. "Shall I call the conservation officer for you?"

He raised his brows and nodded. "Tell him I'll meet him down at the dock with the gator." He turned to his granddaughter. "Katie, you drive me down."

"I'll call him right away." Bev had a feeling she knew Kevin from somewhere, and people in this town of less than two thousand weren't that hard to forget. Most of them had come here out of necessity two generations ago to work at shucking oysters, building marinas, and anything else that pertained to fishing and establishing restaurants and shopping areas. Even so, while his dimples had paraded before her with a red warning flag, he looked older than she, and she might never remember who he was.

The girl seemed familiar, too. Her auburn hair tightened back into a ponytail, a tendril curling at the nape of her neck, and the cowlick in her bangs on the left side of her forehead reminded Bev of someone. Nevertheless, trying to remember the person wasn't the most important thing on her mind. She shrugged the memory lapse off and walked back into the lanai. No sense working too hard to remember a jaded past.

She sank back into her chair, picked up her bag, and dug for her phone. After she called the conservation department to come get the gator, she searched through the straw basket of magazines on the floor for something to browse to calm her down after that unexpected visit from Kevin. She settled on an old Lake Serenade coffee-table book that held a hundred pages of photos of Florida's lakes and tropical plants.

The worn flannel shirt Huff had worn so often was draped across the back of his chair. She reached for his shirt, draped it around her shoulders, and leaned back with the opened book on her lap. The shirt still smelled like him.

Huff hadn't judged her for the mistakes in her life. He'd swept her off her feet at a time in her life when she had dismissed any chance of happiness. Nevertheless, her beloved Huff was with the Lord. His death anniversary was today—his fifth. She'd never thought she could let him go—until she met Kevin.

Kevin jockeyed the golf cart around ruts and gaping holes in the road and chuckled to himself while picturing Bev dressing up a gator. The woman had a sense of humor besides good looks. "It's about time they did something to this road. I can barely navigate these ruts in the dark."

Katie gripped the metal roll bar that held up the canopy as she jostled in her seat. "Gramps, why didn't you let me tell her you owned this park and the restaurant?"

He pulled the cart to the side of the road and into the grass as a car coming from behind flashed his lights. Kevin waited till the car passed and wondered how out of all the places he and Katie could have explored today he chose the park where the stunning waitress lived. "What makes you think I wouldn't let you tell her?"

"Come on, Gramps, I'm not dumb. You stopped me in mid-sentence and didn't let me talk about the restaurant."

Kevin pulled the cart back on the road. "I don't want to stir up any curiosity or anger with any of the workers at the restaurant, and I don't see any sense in her knowing I own the park. I just signed the papers for the restaurant. I don't want to inflict angst in one of the employees yet. She'll find out, in time, with the rest of them."

"I thought you told me keeping secrets wasn't wise. She seemed so nice."

He winced. Katie knew how to be direct, just like her mother, but Katie had a softer side to her than Jenny did. "The ownership is not a secret, Katie. I think I'm wiser to approach the situation in this manner. If I tell one person tonight, then by tomorrow, the community gossip line will wrench this thing all out of shape. No one will know the truth or my plan for the business."

"What is your plan?"

Kevin slowed at the Yield sign and turned right to head into town by following the curve of Lake Serenade. "My plan is to make cuts wherever I can, rejuvenate the diner to make the old place more modern, and give the interior some new life. The former owner is selling the diner because it has lost its appeal and a lot of customers. He was losing money."

"Maybe you should go slow with this. My economics teacher said sometimes the best laid plans can actually be the worst laid plans."

Kevin raised his right hand to her. "Give me five, Katie. I have to congratulate you on that one."

She gave his hand a slap and chuckled. "Gramps! You mean our generations have finally come together? You *never* agree with me."

"I wouldn't go that far, but I have to admit, you have a point. While I didn't much like what I saw the other day, the restaurant still held a bit of charm. I'll take my plans slowly, get everyone's input, and see what happens from there. How does that sound?"

She snuggled close to him and looped her arm in his. "I love you, Grandpa. I think this is going to be the best time of my life so far. Who would ever guess that my dad dying would turn into a summer vacation spent with you?"

A surge of guilt poured into Kevin's gut. "I'm sorry

you lost him, but I'm glad you're with me. God knows your life has been less than perfect."

Katie let go of Kevin's arm and took hold of her ponytail. She pulled the elastic band from the clump of hair, allowing it to fall to her shoulders, then bent her head over to ruffle her fingers through the mass. She sat back up straight, and her hair drifted down around her shoulders. "I'm okay with all that's happened, Grandpa. When I was finally able to talk about the abuse, I felt freed like I never have before."

Kevin choked back a tear. If only he'd acted sooner when he noticed the bruises on Katie's arms, but he couldn't allow himself back then to think her father or mother had anything to do with the injuries. If only he'd taken the matter into his own hands instead of letting the police handle Carl's rehabilitation. He may have been transformed and still be with them. Instead, he took his own life in a lonely jail cell. *If only I'd prayed more.* "That's good to hear, honey."

"You don't realize how much you helped me. I think because you didn't have anything bad to say about my father—that helped me. Everyone else was tiptoeing around and trying not to mention him. I wanted to talk and include him in my conversation. You let me do that. You really loved him, didn't you?"

The day Kevin and Katie had a conversation about her father was when he had taken her out on a date to the place where they drop ice cream onto a piece of marble, smash the ice cream, and add all your favorite toppings to the mixture. The same day he and Katie had sat devouring their banana split creation, Kevin had made the decision to loosen many of his ties to New York and head south. He had hoped Jenny and Katie would follow, and they did. "I did love him. I'm glad we were able to talk that day."

"You thought she was hot, didn't you?"

"What? Katie! What do you mean by *hot*?" Kevin knew exactly who she was talking about. The green-eyed waitress had a certain charm about her, and of course he noticed any beautiful woman. While he was amazed that Katie had picked up on his thoughts, he still didn't like that teenage lingo—calling a woman *hot*.

"Grandpa, calm down. *Hot* is just an expression my generation uses. Let me rephrase. You thought she was attractive, right?"

He could read between the lines. Katie had been try-ing for months to get him interested in someone, first in New York and now here, but he had to put a stop to her madness before her antics got out of hand.

Millie was all he wanted to think about. He had made a promise to himself that he'd not get entwined with anyone else. The pain of doing so was too great. It felt like he'd just laid the rose on Millie's casket.

Chapter 3

The bomb had gone off in Bev's head about two-thirty in the morning. At least she had trained herself to awaken instead of lying in bed and allowing the deadly picture to flow across her mind like lava down a rocky hill. She'd gotten out of bed and paced, asking the same question over and over: *Why, Lord? Why did he have to die while in Afghanistan?*

Two cups of coffee later, she had reconciled herself to the fact that Huff had loved being in the military. She was his wife. She had followed first his dream of owning his own garden shop, then his desire to join the National Guard, and most importantly his God. Had Huff not rescued her, she'd probably be wandering today. Still, she hated the nightmare and tried everything to keep it from having control over her life.

"Where are you?" Nora lifted Bev's hand from the

pump on the gallon of ketchup. "You've squirted more on the counter than in the bottle."

"Oh! I didn't even notice I was missing the bottle. I guess I was daydreaming."

"You really need to get to bed earlier."

"I went to bed too early but got woke up quicker than I wanted."

"Have the dream again?"

Bev walked around the counter to the sink and squeezed out one of the bleach-soaked dishrags. "I'd call it a nightmare, and I don't know what triggered it."

Nora snatched the rag from Bev's hand and cleaned up the bottle and the excess ketchup on the counter. "You've done real good getting the nightmare out of your mind before. Anything else jolt you the last day or two? Something huge usually sets you off."

Bev and Nora had been like sisters. They both had been raised on catfish and cornbread, had lived in the same neighborhood in the Florida Panhandle, and had traveled to school each day on the same bus. The only thing that had ever separated them was when Nora's family moved away just before high school. Nora finally moved back after she graduated.

"Oh. You know what? I had that little gator in my shed again a couple weeks back. I bet that episode triggered the nightmare. I just don't like the gators, even though I pretended I did."

"Why would you pretend you liked them?"

"No reason." She didn't want to admit she pretended in order to impress Kevin.

"Call the sheriff to get him out?"

"No, didn't need to." Bev screwed the caps on and delivered a ketchup bottle to each table.

"Robert came by and told me he had followed the

gator to my place. Just as he finished telling me, a stranger showed up with his granddaughter in a golf cart." She gathered up some of the square, ceramic containers that held envelopes of sugar and artificial sweetener and carried them back to the counter. "The stranger took care of the gator. He said he was from near here. I think he just moved back into town."

"Was it the gator or the man who messed you up?" Nora opened a box of white sugar packets and began to load the containers. "What'd he look like?"

Bev shot a glance past the female college student who sat at a far table with two open books and a cup of coffee when the front door opened. "Like him."

Nora squinted at the front door. "The man from a few weeks ago?"

"Yep." Bev made her way toward him and his granddaughter.

Nora's muffled comment trailed after Bev. "And you said you weren't interested."

"Bev!" Katie pushed in the door, her flip-flops smacking against the linoleum as she headed for Bev and came to an abrupt stop in front of her.

"Hi, Katie. I'm glad you finally took me up on my offer, although"—Bev pointed to the chrome clock on the wall behind the counter—"it's rather early for soda."

Katie swatted at the gnat flying around her face. "Oh, we're not here for a soda." She looked back at her grandpa, who returned her glance as he sheepishly brought up the rear. Katie's smile disappeared.

Bev took a sidelong glance at Kevin as the upbeat feeling he gave her that first day returned. She glanced back at Katie. "You're not? Then, you must be here for breakfast."

Katie swiveled her head to glare at her grandpa,

turned back to Bev, and wrinkled her nose. She pointed her thumb over her shoulder. "Ask him why we're here. I'm evidently not allowed to comment."

Bev could relate. She'd had a few of her own episodes with her mother and father. Obviously, the air was less than friendly between Katie and her grandfather. However, Bev wasn't inclined to take sides. He deserved the benefit of the doubt. "Kevin," she pulled one of the chairs out from the table. "Care to have a seat? Would you like a cup of coffee?"

He placed his hand next to hers on the chair back, gave off an air of innocence, and motioned for her to sit down. "Yes, I'll have a seat. No, I had my quota of coffee this morning. May I ask you to join me?"

Bev took a glance at Nora, waited for an affirmation, and shrugged her shoulders. Nora nodded knowingly and went back to filling sugar containers. "Looks like the boss gives her go-ahead. I can for a short time. The lunch crowd will pick up soon."

"She's the boss?"

"Just for a while. All the employees voted her second-in-command since our real boss hasn't shown up for weeks."

"Then, why don't you have a seat in this chair?"

"Thank you, I will." After she settled into the chair, she noticed Katie out of the corner of her eye. She had made herself at home by helping Nora place the sugar packets into the chrome holders.

His hands remained on the back of the chair until Bev had comfortably positioned it under the table. "Thank you."

"All situated?"

Bev nodded, and he took the chair across from her. Katie showed up at their table with one of the containers of sugar, and the air grew tense again. She set it down next to the mustard and ketchup with more than a gentle landing. "Don't mind me. I'm just working." She gave her grandpa a smirk before leaving.

Bev narrowed her brows. "Is everything okay? I get the feeling she's not too happy with you today."

Kevin took one of the sugar packets out and patted his fingers against the edge while he maneuvered the packet around in his hand. "She's not. She and I have differing views on things. She'll get over it. I told her I was going to break some news to you today."

"What news would you have for me? We don't even know each other."

"We do know each other *slightly*." His mirthful eyes put her at ease as he appeared to ponder his words. He quieted his voice to a whisper. "I'm the new owner here, Bev. Didn't you know that Tom would sell at some point?"

Bev let out an audible moan and leaned back in her chair. "The *new* owner?" Lake Serenade was more than amiable to new visitors, but residents didn't take well to outsiders coming in and making changes. She doubted he'd have an easy time switching over. "Your purchase explains why Tom hasn't shown up for work. None of us could figure out what happened."

"I'd hoped Tom would have called a meeting of all his employees by now. Sadly, I heard this morning he left town yesterday. I'm left with the burden of calling the meeting now, and I hoped that you might be willing to help me set the scene with the employees." He maintained his eye contact as he lowered his head.

Every bone in her body turned to gelatin, and her throat went dry. She and every other employee in the restaurant were at the mercy of this hunk of a man sitting across from her. One shouldn't be attracted to one's boss. How could she work for him? Kevin wasn't like plain ol' Tom. He was a...a *man*. "Kevin, since you're my new boss, I feel that I should call you by your last name, which is... ?"

"Please, just call me Kevin." He inhaled deeply as if he were getting ready for another bombshell then let his breath out slowly. "Shall I continue?"

She leaned forward with her arms on the table and settled her heels on the chrome bar that stretched from one front leg of the chair to the other. Tom had given her this job out of sympathy. She needed to earn as much as possible to supplement the income she received from Huff's retirement, and Tom had been there for her. "Kevin, can I be frank with you? I don't think the employees are going to give you a happy reception. None of us knew anything about this. Oh yes, we knew he'd eventually retire, but ten years down the road, not now. Tom's been good to every single soul he employs."

"I'm aware of Tom's benevolence, Bev. He told me as much."

"And why did you pick me to tell? You put me in an awkward position."

He fixed his gaze on her. "I hadn't intended on talking to anyone before I called all the employees together, but you and I had a chance meeting. Katie helped me to realize that it was no accident that we happened to be riding around the lake when we noticed you in distress. I agree with her. Will you help me?"

She returned his stare. "I don't know, Kevin. Are we going to lose our jobs?"

"I simply want to talk with everyone. I haven't made any plans. The more I've thought about restructuring, the more I think I need to talk with each of you before I make any announcements."

Bev looked around to Nora and Katie deeply engrossed in a conversation then turned back around and looked Kevin in the eye. She didn't want to be nice. She didn't want to talk to him. She didn't want him to be her boss. *Lord, please help me make the right decision here.*

"Okay, Kevin, I'll call the meeting for two weeks from tonight. That would be July twenty-eighth. The restaurant closes at eight o'clock. All our current employees will already be here on account of the busy supper hour. We serve all-you-can-eat oysters that night, and nearly everyone in town comes out for the meal."

He appeared pleased and leaned forward on the table, a platinum cross on a brown cord swinging out from the V-neck opening of his striped, gauze shirt. "You'll never know how much your decision relieves me, Bev. I'll be back at eight, two weeks from tonight."

"Wait, you can't just come in here, scare me half to death by telling me you bought this restaurant, and then leave. What am I going to say to everyone? Now that I know, how can I keep the meeting secret?"

"The meeting is only a secret if you make it one. I know already I can trust your judgment. I'll leave the confidentiality choice up to you."

"I don't know about this."

"Everything will work out. I appreciate your help. On that note, I'll go before anyone wonders why you chose to sit down and talk to me at all." He gave her a nod, and moved the chair away from the table.

Katie headed toward the door behind him. She shrugged her apology to Bev then gave him an improvised smile. "I hope I see you again, Bev—if I'm allowed to."

Bev tried to digest all of Katie's attempts to discredit her grandfather and followed her and Kevin to the door. "Of course you'll see me. Our Sunday school class is going bowling in a few days, if you want to go. Also, I was thinking maybe we could have that soda together tomorrow afternoon. Is that a good time?"

Katie stopped at the door and turned around. "I would be disappointed if we couldn't."

Kevin held the door open and beamed fondly at Katie. "I think you have this young girl wrapped around your finger, Bev. I'm sure she's looking forward to spending more time with you."

Katie fell silent and walked past Kevin out the door. Kevin exchanged a look of futility with Bev then followed Katie out.

Bev had wanted to ask him more questions about the whole transition, but he evaded them by his quick exit. Why was he so confusing? One minute he was full of charm and the next, mystery. Obviously suave when he made business decisions, he seemed lacking in the art of social graces. He'd hurried out the door with not even a thank you. What did she expect? He didn't owe her anything, and she didn't know if she wanted him to.

A yearning, an ache so deep that Bev couldn't identify it, wormed its way into her heart and soul as soon as Katie was out of sight. Even so, Bev sensed a change in the wind's direction—a change in which a young girl, Katie Johnson, was about to deliver to this childless woman a decent summer. Maybe, in turn, she could figure out this Kevin whatever-his-last-name-was.

Chapter 4

"How are you coming, kiddo?" Kevin squeezed a marble-sized pool of 30 SPF suntan lotion into his palm then held out the tube to Katie. He'd talked himself blue about her protecting her fair skin in the Florida sun, but she'd fought him every step of the way.

She shook her headful of red curls, tactfully took the tube, and set it on the placemat. "I don't need lotion. I have oily skin." Katie situated three blue plastic tumblers into the picnic basket next to the jars of spicy mustard and barbecue sauce, already nestled among the red cloth napkins and tartan plaid throw.

Kevin rubbed his hands together until the lotion was evenly distributed then wiped it across his fore-head, nose, and cheeks. He wiped the excess on his arms then picked the tube up, took hold of Katie's hand, and planted the tube in her palm. How did one tell a teenager precisely what one wanted without casting a shadow on the entire day? "Remember our little talk about the sun?"

"You told me Florida was not like Ticonderoga, where my biggest problem was keeping the sun blush from my face as I skied down Grossman's Mountain."

"And?"

She expelled a puff of air. "Oh, all right. I guess I can appease you in this one matter." She dropped to the caned chair near the table and rolled the already-short-enough shorts up a half inch. She opened the tube and squeezed some of the lotion into her hand then handed the tube to Kevin. "Mom never makes me do this stuff."

Kevin pressed out more lotion then applied it on his neck, arms, and the backs of his knees. "That's okay, Katie, Mom isn't here to tell you, but I am. This is Florida, not New York, and as long as you're here, I'll preach to you about the glories and the dangers of the sun overhead." He wasn't about to give Katie a checkered flag to the world of skin cancer like his sister Anita had. "Now, let me ask you a question. Why three glasses?"

As soon as she had finished applying the last bit of lotion to her legs, she headed for the window and stared across the road. "I thought we might ask Bev to go along."

"Bev? I don't mind if you spend time with her, but why don't just you and I enjoy the day together? You've already met with her two times this past week."

"I prefer her to Hattie Lincoln. I don't care for Hattie that much. She's a little too pushy for me."

He headed over to put his arm around Katie and to gently lead her back to the tube of lotion she left open on the wooden table. "Do that double on your face, arms, and shoulders. You'll thank me one day. For your information—or should I talk in your terms—FYI, I'm not into Hattie either. I've known of her through personal acquaintances, and Hattie is just a whimsical eccentric in every area of her life. She does what she wants, but she is a very amiable person. She has a lot of decorating ideas I think we can use at the restaurant."

"I'm a woman, Grandpa. I read between her lines. She has a bigger motive than what you think."

"Hattie already has someone she's interested in down the coast." Kevin knew where Katie was headed. She wanted Bev in their lives. He could tell the first day Katie met Bev that they were kindred spirits. "Okay, to satisfy this turmoil you're in because of my relationships, let's head over to the diner and see what Bev has planned after she's off work. If she agrees to go with us, I'll put to death any chance of Hattie intruding into my life—except for decorating. Sound okay?"

Katie squeezed the lotion into her palm, rubbed both palms together, and slicked the lotion around and down both arms. "I'm swimming in this stuff just for you. Does that answer your question? Please do my back." She gave him a coy smile.

"I'll do your back, but you do triple on your exposed skin around that…that handkerchief of a T-shirt you have on."

Katie moaned. "Gramps, this is called a halter top, and everyone wears them."

"Not if I have anything to say about it. Now hurry and get your things. Since we're going to Bev's, I need to stop at the lumberyard."

"What for?"

"You'll see."

The huge gap in the bottom of the shed where the ground showed chewed, uneven holes caught Bev's attention as she pulled her white sedan into the drive. The shed wasn't the only thing that needed fixing. The car had over 147,000 miles on the speedometer and needed a new battery and fuel pump. Nevertheless, the clunker still ran and provided transportation to and from work. She turned off the motor and got out of the car.

However, she refused to let anything get her down. She lived in a virtual garden of blooms. She'd always looked forward to the first turn on her street when she could see carpets of blossoms from down at the lake. The flowers surrounded both sides of her carport and outlined the ground around the lanai.

Bev's coreopsis already stood tall at three feet and produced copious early orange and yellow flowers. However, the dramatic, butterfly like petals of her snapdragons, which grew across the outside front of the lanai, were her favorites.

Nevertheless, flowers don't grow unless one cares for them. The temperature had already climbed to the low nineties, and the four o'clock sun beat down on the flowers, causing them to droop. Bev snatched her pruners from the canvas pouch hanging just inside her lanai door and clipped off about a dozen of them to display in the house. The rest would perk up when the sprinklers came on in the early morning.

She headed back inside and laid the flowers on the kitchen counter. When she came back out to replace the pruners in the pouch, her breath caught in her throat when a familiar van came up the grade. *Oh no, it's Kevin and Katie. I'm a mess.*

They had barely pulled up before Katie jumped out and hurried to the door. "Are you busy?"

Bev felt a trickle of sweat run down the back of her

head. *So much for trying to impress Kevin.* She offered a polite smile. "Don't worry about it. Come in."

Kevin got out and walked around the front of the van but stopped short of walking to the door. His eyes met hers. "Why don't we give you a moment, and we can come back."

Katie shot him a look of dismay. "Gramps, it's okay."

Had Kevin noticed Bev's desperate look of anguish when she'd realized she looked a mess?

Bev opened the door wider and motioned to him. "You see the real me, once again. Come on in and have a seat out here on the lanai. I'll just go freshen up a bit."

He pointed to the shed. "I have a better idea, if you don't mind."

Katie stepped inside while Bev went out the door. "What's your idea?"

Kevin opened the back door of the van and retrieved the lumber he'd purchased and a rusted metal toolbox. "I should get the hole in the bottom of your shed repaired in no time. Just keep in mind; I'm only repairing the bottom. I'll come back another time and replace the rest of the boards."

Bev beamed. "Thank you so much. I'll just head inside and get ready."

She walked back into the lanai, where Katie checked out her hanging plants. "This is beautiful in here. My grandma used to have basketfuls of petunias on her porch up north." She folded up the edges of each leg on her shorts. "By the way, don't freshen up too much. We came to ask you to go on a picnic with us. You'll just get hot again."

"A picnic sounds like fun." She glanced at the shed where Kevin had already stripped away the bottoms of three wide boards.

Katie pointed out front. "Your snapdragons out front are beautiful, but they're a little bit limp. Do you want me to water them?"

"Those will get watered later. I'm getting ready to put some of them in a vase, if you'd like to arrange them for me." Bev reached over to get Huff's shirt and rolled it into a ball. On the way by the washer, she threw the shirt in.

"Will do." Katie followed Bev into the kitchen.

Bev pointed to the cabinet under the sink. "I have a slender glass vase under there. You can fill it about half full with water and arrange the flowers I've laid here on the countertop."

"I'll have them all ready by the time you come back out."

"Thanks! I'll go and freshen up…less than a bit since we're going on a picnic." Bev winked at her before she headed to her bedroom.

This invitation caught her off guard, but the thought of having such a pleasant evening energized her. Bev hadn't had a personal date for years. Here she was at her worst—dirt under her nails and grease from the diner in her hair—and they still wanted her to go on an outing with them.

While Katie searched for the vase for the flowers, Bev hurried across to her bedroom to get ready. After closing the door behind her, she made a beeline for the bathroom. *I don't care if I'll sweat again. I have to start off clean.*

The quickest shower on record ensued as she yanked two Turkish towels from the shower curtain rod and positioned one on top of the throw rug by the tub and dropped the other on top of the first.

She turned the silver control knob to full blast and

stepped into her tub. She quickly covered her hair with a shower cap, pulled up the lever to start the shower, and scrubbed down in record time before the hot water had even filtered through the pipes.

After she blotted her feet on one towel and wrapped the other around her body, she flitted across the bare floor to the carpet of her bedroom. With the speed of an angry hornet, she threw together an outfit of white cropped pants, light blue tank top, and dark blue, gauze shirt to wear over the tank top. She still managed to dot her face with a smudge of foundation. Leaving a littered trail of clothes and towels behind her, she slipped her feet into some navy wedge sandals and reached for the doorknob just as she heard glass crashing to the floor.

"Oh no! Bev, I'm sorry." Katie didn't hide the despair in her voice as it reverberated past the thin walls in the mobile home to Bev's bedroom. Then she heard Kevin.

"That's okay, take your time. I'm finished outside, and I've got cleanup in here under control."

Bev didn't want to rush out and embarrass Katie, so she went back to the bathroom and applied a little eye shadow, eyeliner, and a smudge of blush. As she pondered her timing, she sat down on the edge of the bed.

She really liked Katie and Kevin both and could see herself developing a genuine friendship with them. She'd had a couple meetings with Katie, but a picnic outing would give her a chance to get to know both of them better. When she thought Katie and Kevin might be finished sweeping up the glass, she headed out the door.

"We had a slight accident out here with your vase, Bev." Kevin popped up from behind the counter as Bev walked out. Katie had the broom in hand while Kevin held the dustpan.

"I'm sorry, Bev," said Katie. "I dropped the vase. I hope you don't mind I snooped around for your broom. I saw you with it during the gator incident, so we searched the most likely places. I wanted to have the mess cleaned up before you came out."

Bev hoped a sunny smile would calm things. She proceeded around the counter where Kevin stood with his dustpan full of glass shards. "Let me show you where to dispose of the glass." She opened the small closet next to the sink and pointed to the plastic-lined wastebasket, and then turned to Katie. "I could give you a hug. I hated that vase. Every time I used it, I was reminded of the circumstance I was in when I purchased it."

Katie wiped the moisture from her forehead. "Really?"

"Really. I had gone to the store to get a different pair of gardening gloves one day. Then I noticed the vase in the discount aisle. I tucked it under my arm on my way to the checkout. I laid the gloves on the conveyor, got a ten-dollar bill from my purse, and paid for them. Neither the clerk nor I noticed the vase. Wouldn't you know I got stopped by the beeper as I left the store?"

Kevin emptied the glass into the basket, closed the door, and flashed a guarded smile to Bev. "You mean we've taken up with a common thief?"

Bev drummed her fingers on the counter and stared him down. "I can only tell you I won't shoplift again." She looked away, picked up a pan of brownies sitting on the back of the stove, and held them up to Kevin. "Anyone for double-chocolate brownies? My guilt-ridden conscience over baking them in the first place would thank you."

Kevin turned on the faucet. "Give me a moment here

to wash my hands. I better be in charge of those just so your conscience doesn't get the better of you again." After he tore off a section of paper towel and dried his hands, he took the pan from her.

"Come on, Bev, before he charms you out of any more food," said Katie. "You've just made Grandpa's day with those brownies. He loves sweets, and I'm not a baker."

Kevin followed Katie out the door while Bev made a final round of the house to make sure she'd turned off everything. "I guess I'm finally ready. I hope you two aren't starving."

After she closed the lanai door behind her, she inserted the key into the door. Before she could turn the lock into place, Kevin walked over and took the key from her. "I'll get this."

In the process, his hand brushed against hers. While she wasn't sure those chills should have gone through her skin at his touch, she felt somehow connected to him because of the contact. Katie strolled into Bev's line of vision on the other side of Kevin and gave her an obvious wink. Heat flashed across Bev's face, and she silently warned Katie with pursed lips and a wrinkled brow.

Had Kevin meant to touch her hand, or was the graze accidental? While embarrassed to admit a spark flickered gently within her, she also wondered if she could fan the spark into flame. Suddenly, her hundred reasons for staying away from this man had dwindled to zero.

Chapter 5

Bev seemed familiar to him, as if he'd met her in the past. Even if he could remember, he'd not mention the fact because his hasty departure from Lake Serenade years ago was meant to erase the town's memory of him and Millie, not stimulate it.

"Didn't you, Gramps?" Katie sat behind Kevin and Bev in the van and tugged her seat belt as far as it would go so she could see through the gap between the two front seats.

"Hmm?" Kevin caught Katie's reflection in his rearview mirror just in time to see her frown at him. Luckily for Kevin, Katie had the gift of conversation and could fill in, in an area where he had no talent. "Repeat that, honey."

"The worms you and I dug up behind your house in the Adirondack's. I told Bev you got in big trouble when you decided to store them in Grandma's fridge."

"Do you have to remind me? She didn't forgive me for days." He glanced at Bev. He felt comfortable with her. One would have thought she'd known the family forever by the way she interacted with them both. "I guess her anger had something to do with the dirt spilling out when I took them back out of the thing."

Bev chuckled. "My dad always kept his containers of bait in a cooler out in our garage. He insisted we could pack our food in, once the worms were gone. Needless to say, my mother couldn't stomach his idea."

He liked her laugh, polite and graceful yet engaging. Her sense of humor, much like Katie's, was charming. He suddenly pictured himself at the diner meeting and hoped she'd still be friendly toward him. "Where else are we supposed to put bait?"

"Gramps, tell Bev about the first time Mom and Dad met." Katie unhooked her seat belt and leaned up against the back of Bev's seat. "Wait till you hear this, Bev. You'll love the story."

Kevin cleared his throat. He wasn't one to reminisce too much about his family's background, and he didn't think the story funny. One of the most heartbreaking times in his life had been when his little girl took up with a complete stranger. One day he was holding her in his arms, and the next, he had to watch someone else hold her. "We lived out on Long Island, back then. Katie's mother—"

"Jenny, Bev. Her name's Jenny," said Katie.

"Yes," he continued, "Jenny was quite a tomboy. She spent almost all her after-school hours on the dock casting out crab traps into the water and bringing home dinner. While other teenage girls would spend their time looking in mirrors, buying new makeup, and talking about their latest flame, Jenny would find joy in heading back down to the docks in the early morning and trapping her own bait before she caught the bus to go to school."

Bev adjusted her position to face Kevin. "I've done all kinds of things like that down here, including shucking oysters. Sometimes, being a tomboy is good. At least that way you don't get so caught up in the unimportant things in life. So when did her husband enter the picture?"

Katie grabbed Kevin's shoulder. "This is the best part; isn't it, Gramps?"

Kevin caught a glimmer of laughter in Bev's green eyes as he took a quick look in her direction. "That depends on what viewpoint you're taking. We lived out on Long Island back then, in a decrepit addition of homes that bordered the commuter track heading into New York City, where he came from. He hopped off a train because Jenny stood in the backyard waving at him. Katie thinks her mother's story is romantic, but we've told her over and over how dangerous a similar situation would be today. Even then, Millie and I were furious."

"I'm not dumb," said Katie. "I wouldn't do what Mom did."

"I know you're not dumb, but a similar situation today would be sure death," he said.

"You're too protective." Katie sat back against her seat, pulled the shoulder belt under her arm, and clicked her belt over her waist. "You have to look at some things from a romantic point of view and not a grandfather's point of view."

Kevin looked up in his rearview mirror at her. "I'm smart, not protective."

Katie glared back at him. "Is that why you made me change my shirt? It's an absolutely scorching day out, and I'm stuck in this gray shirt with the statue of liberty smeared all over the front."

Kevin looked away from the mirror and kept his eyes straight ahead. Inviting a second opinion from another woman might put his life at risk, but he couldn't help himself. "What do you think, Bev? Did Jenny make a dangerous choice?"

Bev's sterling silver charm bracelet jingled in front of his face and pointed toward the parking lot. "I think we should pull into that available spot over in the far row while we have the chance. The beach will only get more crowded as the day gets closer to sunset, and I want to make sure I have a crack at the good-smelling food packed inside Katie's picnic basket."

Kevin made a wild lurch around the lot to the next row of parking. "As you wish."

After Bev unclicked her seat belt, she reached behind her to pat Katie on the knee. "You must have worked all morning on your food."

Kevin smirked. "I see you're not going to allow me to wrangle you into expressing your opinion."

Bev shook her head. "No chance, Kevin."

Katie revived from her pouting as she undid her seatbelt. "Thanks for the compliment about my picnic, Bev. My gift is actually making the basket look good. I just made a few sandwiches and brought along a couple kinds of crackers to go with them. Okay?"

"That sounds delicious."

Kevin angled the van into the parking spot and turned off the motor. "I'm looking forward to those brown—" The front car door opened and closed as the sliding back door rumbled open. Katie grabbed the picnic basket, got out, and pushed the button to close the automatic door.

He chuckled to himself. Bev seemed to be every bit as much of a kid as Katie as they conferred outside the van. He liked the way Katie had taken so quickly to Bev. Katie wasn't prone to take to anyone new, but she needed a woman in her life. He reached under his seat for his fishing hat, shoved it on his head, and got out of the car. "Wait up, you two."

"Lead the way, Bev," said Katie. "Come on, Gramps. Let's hurry over to the vacant area under the two palms."

Within seconds, the women had meandered past the parking lot and onto the grass and sand area of the beach. He clicked his key fob to lock the car doors and headed off to join them. Suddenly, he was glad he had ignored the realtor's advice not to purchase the diner. Returning to Lake Serenade might not be so bad after all.

Katie lifted the red plaid blanket out of the basket. "Here, Bev. Would you do the honors? I'll get the other stuff out."

"I'd be happy to." She unfolded the blanket, held the edges, gave a flap in the air, then watched the blanket float evenly to the ground.

Just as the blanket settled, a gust of wind flipped one of the corners. Kevin rushed up to secure the opposite side. "Guess I was needed around here for something. I was beginning to think you ladies would prefer to do your dining alone."

Bev had noticed the quick wink he gave usually accompanied a quip or sarcasm. Whatever his reason for winking, the gesture added dimension to his serious side and gave her a reason to think he liked her. Before today's invitation, she viewed him as an overzealous business owner trying to impose his new ideas on a group of people who only wanted to keep their jobs. After only a couple of hours in his company, she'd seen a fun-loving side. "We only wanted to lay claim to our plot of land out here. I told Katie this area is usually the first to fill with picnickers, even during the week."

Katie had her back to them as her attention drifted to a group of teenagers down near the water. Her escape was inevitable, and Kevin was right on her departure. "You're not thinking of going down to the water, are you?"

"I'll be right back, guys. You go ahead without me. Brian from the surf school's down there." She looked at Bev. "I met him at a get-acquainted dealy at some church my grandpa wanted me to go to."

Katie scurried off, and Bev eyed the young man Katie called Brian. Bev had seen him before when a group of young people hung out in front of the diner. He was a clean-cut guy, but Bev could tell by his looks and demeanor he had other things in mind for Katie and was far too old for her.

From the conversations of the girls she taught in her Sunday school class, Bev had learned the guy was pretty well known for his fancy cars, talented surfing down on the Gulf, and quick moves on unsuspecting teenage girls. "Kevin, I don't want to scare you, but I'd watch her around that guy, if I were you."

Kevin leaned on one of the palm trunks and shaded his eyes with the other hand. "I've already been watching them both. She's only known him for a few days, and he's getting a little too close for comfort." He motioned to the blanket. "We might as well sit down. May I interest you in a choice seat facing the water?"

Bev settled down on the blanket, tucked her legs

under her, and faced the beach. "Has he been coming around much?"

Kevin sat down next to her and moved the picnic basket in front of them. "Her cell phone was more of a problem than his being there. I finally took it away. The guy's been texting her until midnight each night. She hasn't dated very much. She has no idea what this character's up to." Kevin lifted out a glass and napkin and gave them to Bev then took the same out for himself.

"Sounds like you have a pretty good grip on things."

He gave her a side glance. "I'm a man, Bev. I used to be a teenager. This guy is up to no good, but if I intervene the way I want to, I'll only push Katie closer to him. I'm trying to be patient."

Bev reached into the basket and removed the napkin covering up the sandwiches. "Oh, the sandwiches are lovely. Katie did a great job. I never would have put together something that decent for a picnic. I fixed peanut butter sandwiches and pickles on my picnics as a kid. Where did she get such talent for creativity? Her mother?"

Kevin stared sullenly out toward the beach where Katie and Brian were wading in the water. "He's holding her hand."

Bev glanced up from the basket and looked down toward the beach then turned back to Kevin. "She's right in front of us, Kevin. What can he do?"

He scowled as he took one of the sandwiches, handed it to Bev, then took another and began to unwrap the plastic. "Jenny was right in front of me, too, when Carl came along. That kid, Brian, sort of reminds me of him. He was unshaven, had a guitar slung across his shoulder, and arrived in our backyard like a wrapped-up present for Jenny. Liked to scare me and Millie to death. Jenny took up with him as she often did with the down-and-outers. As they say, the rest is history."

Bev had to admit, she was concerned about Katie and Brian. Hadn't she thought she had all the answers when she was Katie's age? She knew how quickly things could change and blow up in your face. She also realized the payback for being so carefree. She looked into his eyes. "May I choose to believe that Katie won't run off with him?"

"How can you be so sure?"

"Because she has a good head on her shoulders. I think you can trust her on her decisions. If you want, I can spend some time with her, too. I have numerous activities at my church I can engage her in during the summer." Bev took her sandwich apart, whispered a silent thanks for her food, and reached for the mustard.

He stared adoringly and covered her hand with his. "You have my permission."

After she looked up at him, he gently moved his fingertips across the top of her hand as he drew his hand away.

"Spending time with her will be fun." Bev held up the mustard. "Want some?"

He shook his head then took a bite of his sandwich. "Don't like mustard."

Bev poured some onto her bread and spread it around with the other piece. "Is your daughter back in New York?"

"No, nothing like that. She has some project she's working on up in Tallahassee. Says she may take a couple months to finish her research. I go back and forth with her absence. Sometimes, I wish she were back here raising her daughter, and sometimes I don't. All she and Katie do is fight anyway." Kevin straightened at the sight of Katie walking toward him. "This ought to be good."

"I don't want to intrude, but God has a way of working these things out."

"What do you mean?"

She shrugged. "We pray, and He answers."

"I'm not so sure God is listening to me anymore. If I could see Him do something in Jenny and Katie's lives, I'd never doubt Him again. I don't see anything changing though."

"Katie," said Bev, "come join us. These sandwiches are glamorous and delicious."

Long-faced, Katie sat down next to Bev with her back to the beach. "I saw them in a food magazine and decided to try my hand at them. I can do pretty much anything if I have a pattern to follow."

Bev reached over and placed her palm against Katie's cheek. "You're warm, honey, and I don't think it's from the sun. Are you feeling alright?"

Katie pulled a corner of the blanket over her lap and fiddled with the fabric. She looked once back over her shoulder then back at Bev. "I'm fine. I just got a little frenzied on the beach, and now I'm chilled."

Bev looked at Kevin. "I think Katie may have a fever. Maybe we should end our picnic so you can get her back home in bed. You don't want the fever turning worse."

Kevin leaned toward Katie and rested the back of his hand against her forehead. "Well, maybe Bev's right. Let's get you back home where you can rest awhile. If you don't feel better in the morning, we'll take you to the health clinic in town."

Katie stood to her feet. "Whatever. I'll wait for you two over by the van. Can I have the keys so I can get in?"

Kevin picked up the key fob from the blanket and

tossed it to her. "There you go. We'll gather the things and follow you to the van."

Katie hit the automatic start on the fob and headed toward the van.

Bev had moved to her knees and had already started gathering up the napkins, glasses, and remaining sandwiches. She packed everything back in the basket and closed the lid. "Poor thing. She was so excited about today."

Kevin reached out his hand and took Bev's. "Here, let me help you up." After he drew her to her feet, he hesitated for a moment while he looked into her eyes.

She met his gaze while they still held hands. "Katie… she's waiting."

"Right." He let go of her hand while Brian, interacting with two other girls, drew Kevin's attention to the water. "Maybe Katie's faking being sick. Something makes me wonder if she knew Brian was going to be here."

Bev handed the picnic basket to Kevin and then shook out the blanket. She folded it back into a square and tucked it under her arm. "You worry too much. I don't know Katie very well, but I know her well enough to know she's a grown woman. I believe she knows more about life than you give her credit for."

Kevin paused and turned to face her. His pained expression warned of bad news to come. "She knows too much about life, Bev. She had a father who…"

Bev felt the color drain from her face as she took hold of Kevin's arm. Her imagination took her to places she didn't want to go—not anymore. "Please don't tell me he abused her."

Kevin nodded. He walked a little further then stopped. "He wasn't sexually abusive, but he did hurt her physically on many occasions. He took his life before I had a chance to help him." He leaned his head toward hers and whispered, "She never felt her father's love."

A lengthy conversation ensued as Kevin elaborated on Katie's situation with her father. Eventually, he set the basket down and got the blanket back out. He spread it on the ground for them both to sit on. Bev listened carefully to every word until Kevin indicated they should go. She calmly touched his shoulder. "You never know what scars a person wears, do you?"

After they got back to the van and inside, he met Bev's gaze, and briefly she touched his shoulder. Then, she turned to look at Katie, who had fallen asleep in the back. She shuddered and massaged the first two fingers on her right hand. Arthritis had settled in to the two digits where they hadn't healed correctly. She and Katie had more things in common than she realized.

Chapter 6

Kevin pulled into Bev's drive and turned off the van's lights. "I'll walk you to the door and check out the inside."

"Check out the inside? You don't even have to walk me up. I'll be fine." She'd lived here long enough to know the security at the front gate was excellent. No one in this park had ever had any problems with loiterers. Nevertheless, she suddenly realized gentlemen did this for ladies.

He unclicked his seatbelt. "A woman out after dark in Florida shouldn't have to come home to an empty house." He gave her a nod. "Right?"

"Sure." *You better snatch this one up, Bev. His kind doesn't come around very often.*

She kept her eyes on him as he walked around the front of the van to her side. He opened her door and reached for her hand to help her out.

"Thank you, Kevin. You're so kind." As soon as she stepped out, the sliding door on the passenger's side opened, and they released hands.

"Can I come in, too?" Katie rubbed her eyes and headed for the porch door ahead of Bev and Kevin.

"We're not staying, Katie," said Kevin.

"I hope you're feeling better," said Bev. She stuck her hand, still warm from his touch, into her right pocket, pulled out her key, and held it out to him. "It's been awhile since a gentleman has been this chivalrous to me. I think I'd like you to open the door for me, if you don't mind."

He smiled, took the key from her hand, and opened the door. Katie headed in first and plunked down in Bev's chair. "This feels so good. You guys take your time. I'm fine here."

Bev followed her in, ran her hand across Katie's forehead, and then looked back at Kevin.

He shrugged his shoulders and gave Bev the key. "She seems fine now, doesn't she?"

"Katie, do you need a blanket?"

"I think she's already asleep," said Kevin.

"I have a quilt folded in on the dryer." She headed into the laundry room, returned with the quilt, and tucked it around Katie's body. "All snuggled in."

"She looks pretty cozy."

Katie opened her eyes. "I can't sleep while you're talking."

Bev gave her a pat on the head. "I know you weren't planning on staying long, Kevin, but would you and Katie like some tea?"

"Sure. Can I help?"

Katie pulled the cover around her. "None for me."

Bev headed into the house, opened the cupboard, and

took out two glasses and the sugar. She handed him a spoon from the drawer. "I'll let you add your sugar."

"That's all you need me to do?"

Bev smiled as she filled the glasses with ice and poured the tea. "I can do everything else." She handed him one of the glasses.

Kevin spooned the sugar into his tea and stirred. They stood in the small kitchen, each leaning against an opposite cupboard. He drank it half gone then set the glass on the counter. He folded his arms and fixed his gaze on Bev. "Thank you for everything today. Your support regarding Katie helped me."

He seemed to be more relaxed than he was when Brian had showed up at the beach. As he continued to watch her, Bev sipped from her glass wondering what an appropriate amount of time should be spent staring back at him. "She's a sweet girl. You're doing a good job with her."

"You think?"

She struggled to control the nervousness in her voice. "Absolutely."

His breath seemed to catch in his throat as he pointed over his shoulder. "Well, I better get her home and in bed." He started moving toward the kitchen door. "We have a busy day tomorrow."

She followed him out onto the lanai. Katie looked asleep and was bent over the arm of the wicker chair. "She's welcome to stay the night, Kevin. The decision is yours."

Kevin knelt down in front of Katie. "Hey girl. Let's get up and head home. You okay?"

"Huh?"

He helped her to her feet, and she leaned against him. "I think we'll be fine heading home. Besides, I have a lot of work for her to do tomorrow morning. I want to involve her in making a plan for the redecorating for the diner."

"Redecorating? Tom's wife redid everything in the diner not that long ago. What more could you do?"

"After I went over Tom's books and receipts for the diner, I decided to change the appeal of the interior." Kevin scratched his forehead. "The lady you saw with me at the diner was my decorator. She's out of town for a few days, but she's working on a plan also."

"Plan? But I thought from the way you looked over the interior that you were taken by the decorations."

"Don't take this to heart, Bev, but have you ever looked at the interior as a stranger walking in off the street? It's dated. Changes have to be made."

Bev chuckled as she thought about her yellow dress. *If he's going to change anything, please let it be the uniforms.* "Here, I'll get the door for you. I wouldn't tell anyone else you have plans to change the diner just yet."

Katie raised her eyes to Bev before she leaned back on Kevin. "Good night, Bev. Thanks for everything."

Bev closed the door and locked it while she watched Kevin help his granddaughter into the front seat. After he shut the door, he walked back to the lanai door and put his palm against the glass. "I'll see what I can do, Bev. No promises."

No promises? Bev looked up into his face and instinctively pressed her hand against her side of the glass. She stood at the glass as long as he did and stared at him as long as he gazed at her.

The moment was brief, but the imagery was intense. Everything about tonight felt good and right. Nevertheless, no words had been spoken at their parting, no promises were made, but when he left, she knew the man from New York had invaded her heart.

Kevin looked over at Katie asleep against the door. He smiled to himself. What prompted him to put his hand on the glass? She returned the gesture. He'd better make sure he knew what he was doing because he was in no position to trifle with any woman's emotions, let alone one of his employees. If he were honest, she had already become more than an employee.

Would she think badly of him if she knew his past? Only Millie had known his true past. She had partnered with him. Could another woman look past his mistakes, perhaps someone as compassionate as Bev?

He slowed the van and turned into his driveway while mumbling under his breath. "Katie, what have you gotten me into?" He put the van in Park and turned off the motor.

"What, Gramps?" Katie rubbed her eyes and straightened up. "Are we home?"

"We are."

She laid her head back against the headrest and gazed over at him. "I know. I've been awake the whole time we've been driving."

He touched his hand to her chin. "You okay? You seemed a little upset after you finished with Brian today."

She looked into his eyes as hers filled with tears. "I was, and I am."

"Katie-girl, whatever happened to all those times we used to talk for hours?"

Katie turned away. "I grew up, Gramps, and you've changed, too. I'd still love to talk; I just think twice before I tell you anything that might upset you. You have enough things on your mind."

"I've tried to be there for you, honey, even from the first time you fell off your tricycle and everyone else told you to get up and try again. All I did was cuddle you."

"I remember."

"If you need to talk, go ahead. You know you'll feel much better after you've poured your thoughts all out." Kevin pulled his hand back. He'd let too many other issues control him lately. Had she needed him and he hadn't been available for her? As he had learned to do, he would pretend that nothing she said bothered him. He'd pretend to take lightly whatever she revealed, and he wouldn't lay any guilt on her tonight. Even so, Jenny needed to speed up her research and get home to take care of her daughter.

Katie turned and stared out the front of the van. "See the tangled grapevine next door on Mr. Hutchins's cement fence? All the grapes have been harvested. The vine has dried. Every time I come or go from the house, I see the vine. That's what my emotions have felt like since I met Brian."

"What do you mean?"

"I mean, I feel helpless and lifeless. Brian is not the man he portrays himself to be. At first, he drew me in with his exuberance and attentiveness. Everyone seemed to like him, even the adults. When I first saw him at that get-together, he seemed so much like my father. Something clicked, and I fell for him."

"Katie, I hate to tell you this, but not enough time has passed for you to fall for him."

"I told myself there hadn't been enough time when he started pressuring me. Then, last night—don't get mad,

Gramps—he showed up down in the yard below my bedroom window. He started throwing pebbles against the glass to get my attention."

Kevin put his hand on the door handle. *What do you think you're going to do, Kevin, run away so you don't have to listen?* "Maybe I don't want to know what happened next." He hadn't heard anything last night, and she couldn't have crawled out the window or the alarm would have gone off. What had this Brian kid done to make himself so attractive to her?

"I think you'd be proud. I snuck past your room and went out to talk to him."

"You want me to be proud you snuck past my room?" The windows began to fog inside the van, and he turned the ignition on long enough to roll his window down about an inch.

"Wait till I finish, Gramps. The proud part comes next. I couldn't believe he'd ask me to do the things he did. I was scared, actually. I'm not ready to give myself away. I realized, at that point, he wasn't for me. That's when the proud part comes. I told him to get a life and that I couldn't bring myself to do those things with any guy. Then, I did an about-face and left him standing. He didn't even try to change my mind. He just shrugged his shoulders and headed toward his car."

Other than having to identify Carl's body when he died, this was the sickest feeling Kevin had ever experienced. Katie had come so close to disappearing and following in her mother's footsteps, and he didn't even hear her go out the door. "I am. I am proud of you, honey, but why the meeting today?"

"I didn't plan it. He probably went to the beach to pick some other girl up. I don't think he believed me last night. You know how guys are sometimes. You have to hit them over the head before they understand anything. When I saw him at the lake, I knew I had to put an end to our relationship once and for all. Do you know why?"

"To be honest, honey, I don't care why. I'm just glad you ended your friendship."

"Gramps, humor me."

"You're always surprising me, honey. Why?"

"Because of Bev. Since we met together the other day, I've felt different. I've felt like I've known her forever. I think she's someone I can talk to. I don't understand why, but I'd like to spend more time with her. She makes me feel like an adult, yet I feel safe with her. What do you think?"

Now that the steam had cleared from their windows, Kevin started the engine and rolled his window back up. Truth be known, he wanted to see more of Bev also. "If you want to spend more time with her, I'm for that. So far, I trust Bev, and I know she'll be delighted to talk to you and have you around."

Katie tried to play her magic on Kevin with her engaging eye contact, her more-green-than-hazel eyes peering out from underneath those marathon eyelashes. She had a striking resemblance to Jenny. "Don't you want to spend more time with her, too?"

Kevin turned off the engine, pulled the keys from the ignition, and opened his door. He couldn't help but let a smile cross his face. "Don't bat those crazy eyes at me. Let's head in. It's been a long day." He glanced over at the grapevine as he closed his door. He'd had a similar analogy of the vine.

His own life hadn't been so smooth lately. He'd told himself this diner would be his last business venture and then he'd settle down. He'd told himself he had to get right with God and quit playing games. Now Katie wanted to pair him up with Bev. Would a romance be another rocky road to travel down?

Katie reached in the back for the picnic basket, lifted it over the seat, and got out of the van. She followed annoyingly close on his heels. "Okay, here's my take on what just happened. I struck a chord with you, and you'd like to get to know her as much as I would. So why don't you want to talk about her?"

Kevin unlocked the door to the house and rushed to the hallway to disengage the alarm. After he had turned it off, he motioned to Katie. "Close the door so I can set the alarm again."

"What are you afraid of?" Katie pushed the door closed with a little more force than he was comfortable. More than that, she was using more might than necessary to get him to commit to a summer of fun.

"I'm not afraid. The people I bought the house from told me that all types of vandals hang out in the grapefruit grove over across the street. I'm just playing things safe. If I were the only one here I wouldn't care, but I'm not. I'm concerned about you. And how did you get out of the house last night?"

"Okay, first of all, you didn't answer my question. I wasn't talking about the alarm. I meant, what are you afraid of with Bev? At least give her a chance." She smirked. "And about the alarm. I've watched you set the alarm and turn it off. I'm not dumb." Katie locked the door behind her and then set the picnic basket on the dining room table. "So, you have to answer my question about Bev."

Kevin punched in the code then blew Katie a kiss as he walked into the kitchen. "I do like Bev, and the emphasis is on *like*." He opened the refrigerator door and shuffled some bowls around in order to reach the milk. He lifted the foil from one bowl, wrinkled his nose, and set the bowl in the sink. "Should have thrown that chili out days ago."

Katie followed him in. "And continue your comments on Bev, please." Katie removed the foil from the spoiled food, dumped the chili down the garbage disposal, and rinsed out the dish.

"And—" he took out a carton of skim milk, jiggled it to see how much was in it, and closed the door "—I have nothing more to say."

Katie opened the cupboard door and took out two glasses. She set them down on the counter. "Here, I'll take some, too, after you've poured yours. You know, you're not telling me the truth. I saw what you did."

Kevin emptied the remainder of the milk equally into each glass. He gulped his down, put the milk carton into the wastebasket, and then set the glass in the kitchen sink. He knew what she was talking about. He had no idea what had possessed him to make such a gesture, but he couldn't change what he'd already done. "What do you think I did?"

Katie drank her milk while he walked out of the kitchen and into the living room. He heard her turn on the faucet and rinse the glasses out before she followed him into the living room. Knowing Katie wasn't about to leave things lie, he settled into the overstuffed recliner and reached for the remote. If he could at least pretend to be busy when she came in, perhaps she'd leave him alone and go to bed.

Katie took the remote from him as he pointed it toward the television and sat on the sofa across from him. "You like her, Gramps. I hear a tone in your voice. I see hope in your eyes. The final indication to me nearly unglued me. I saw you touch her hand through the glass.

Your gesture was the most romantic thing I've seen in my life. What are you going to do about her?"

Kevin withdrew the remote from her hand and switched on the television. "Not a thing, Katie. I reacted, that's all. I was in one of those caught-up-in-the-tropical-element kind of things. And, if you noticed, I didn't touch her hand. *She* touched mine."

He heard a moan from Katie as she shook her head and made her way across the room to the stairway. "I'd better hear a whole new attitude when I get up tomorrow morning. If you don't follow through on the little *sign* you gave her, you're in big trouble."

Katie didn't need to know. He'd already decided to follow through.

Chapter 7

"What's up with you, girl?" Nora gave Bev a quick hug. "I was worried when I pulled in the drive and saw all the lights on in here."

As Bev sipped her coffee, she thought about the extra pot of coffee she'd consumed the night before. It had kept her up until five o'clock. Her caffeine high barely allowed her an hour to sleep. She didn't need any more. "Nora, I don't know if I even locked my house when I left this morning, but I just decided to come on over here."

Nora put her purse in the employee's locker, unfolded a clean apron from under the counter, and slipped it on. "Well I, for one, am glad you're here. I have some good news and bad news. We're going to have a lot more business this morning because Buzz from the marina is bringing in five fishing buddies of his. He just called me from home."

"And the bad news?"

"Max is coming in an hour late this morning. I just checked the schedule. I forgot he was going to dig for worms this morning with his nephew. On top of that, Buzz said they wanted the house special so that means a lot more work for you and me."

"I'm glad you know all the facets of running this place. I can do anything but cook."

"Follow me." Nora scurried across the kitchen, took two boxes of pancake mix from the shelf, and set them down on the counter. "We have to be ready with un-limited pancakes, sausage, and home-fried potatoes. Coffee is on the house, as always."

Bev set her cup on the counter then stooped down to the lower cupboard to get the utensils necessary to prepare the batter. "See, I knew I had to be here early for some reason."

"You picked a good day to come in. I just hope you can stay alert long enough."

Bev tore the tops off the pancake mix boxes and filled the bowl half full of the mix. "I'll do my best."

Nora clicked on a few buttons underneath the flat-top griddle. "We'll let this heat up while I get the sausage from the back room. What do you think about the meeting tonight?"

The meeting? Bev filled a measuring cup with water and poured it into the bowl. Had Kevin gone ahead and talked to the others already? As far as she knew, only two people were aware of the meeting: her and Kevin. "What meeting are you talking about?"

Nora stopped and turned around. "You don't know?"

Bev started mixing the batter. "I know. Can you tell me how you found out?"

Nora continued to the back room then emerged with

two boxes of sausages. "I hope I don't get anyone in trouble. Wasn't I supposed to know?" She set the boxes next to the griddle.

"Kevin told me, but I didn't think anyone else knew."

Nora turned on the faucet and wet a couple fingers. The water sizzled when she flipped some drops on the hot griddle. "I know because, for some reason, the new owner's granddaughter wanted to spill her guts the other day."

Bev's jaw dropped. "Katie? Maybe I should have told everyone right away. I hadn't planned on you finding out from someone other than me."

Nora ripped the tops from two boxes of sausage. "We'd all know sooner or later. I don't care when I found out." She dumped one box of sausages out on the griddle and spread them evenly apart.

"Nora, I'm terribly worried about what everyone's going to do. Judy can find a job anywhere. She's young and has charisma. Esther might have a problem though. She's got that issue with her back. Tom always worked around her physical issues, but most employers wouldn't. The owner of the Seafood Shack has been after Max to come work with him for a long time. You and I...well, I don't know what we'd do." Bev bit into her bottom lip after her last statement. She was almost certain Kevin wouldn't do anything rash like fire her.

"Bev, you've always told me that God will provide. Will He or won't He? I'm not going to worry if you tell me He'll provide."

"He will. He always has." Bev dumped her coffee down the sink, rinsed out the cup, and then set it near the back. Nora was right. She could never pinpoint a time in her life when God wasn't available for her.

A bizarre sounding blend of automobile horns, some

deep and strong and some sounding like wounded fowl breathing their last breath, came from the parking lot as Buzz pulled in and others followed. Bev peered around the corner to look outside, and Nora followed her. "Oh my, another big day for us, but the neighbors are going to be complaining at that noise."

"Looks like Tom quit the business a little too soon."

"This type of business is fleeting." Nora went for the batter and spooned out six small circles onto the griddle. "I hope we don't run out of food. Feeding this crowd is going to take every single egg we have. I guess there's one good thing about running out."

"What's that?"

"Our receipts. The handsome New Yorker is going to see what a great restaurant this is. I don't think he'll want to fire anyone. Do you?"

"Let's hope not." Bev headed out into the diner to serve water and coffee. The caffeine's edge had begun to wear off, and she found herself yawning as she poured the coffee and thought about the meeting. She knew Kevin would not think of letting her go, but would he let the others stay?

No aspect of business bothered Kevin more than the meeting with the diner employees. He glanced into the mirror above his bureau. "So what is it, Kevin? Are you really worried about impressing all the employees or just the one you spent your evening with last night?" He shook his head and headed for his closet then went back downstairs.

"Which one, Katie?" Kevin held up two ties—one with a deep-blue background and wide, silver diagonal stripes and the other one a solid burgundy red.

Katie laid down her cooking magazine and walked

over to him. "Gramps, how many times have I told you, people in this town don't put on airs? You don't have to be anyone special down here. They'll like you in a pair of blue jeans. Wear those middle-rise, boot-cut ones you got at the fancy men's store in Tallahassee. I love those. Put your blue and gray pin-striped shirt with them, and you'll be ready to go."

"I'm the owner, Katie, not the manager or an employee. I have to present a certain authority, or they won't respect me."

Katie whipped both ties out of his hands. "Trust me on this one. This is not New York City. This is Lake Serenade, Florida. Be normal. They'll love you. You didn't dress up yesterday, and I believe Bev was quite taken with you. And if you just absolutely have to dress up, put your gray gauze shirt on over the pin-striped one."

"Bev?" He'd grown up here and had lost interest, but now, something about the town made him care. He didn't want to upset anyone's plans or dreams. Jobs were hard to come by, and he couldn't bring himself to let any employee go. The best he could do was to explain why he wanted to redecorate and begin remodeling the diner, keep everyone employed, and hope that somewhere along the way business would increase and the diner wouldn't be a loss.

Would he ever have a chance with Bev? He pulled the jeans from a pants hanger and changed into them from the dress pants. He then searched through the myriad of dress shirts packed tightly into the small closet. When he found the pin-striped shirt, he pulled it out. Frowning at the wrinkle in the left sleeve, he exchanged the shirt he had on for the sportier one and then looked again at his image in the mirror. "She *is* the reason you want to look nice, isn't she, Kevin?"

He'd done his research and discovered Bev was a widow. He couldn't fool himself into thinking that he didn't find her attractive, and he was certain she caught the meaning of his gesture the night before. Of course, he knew why he touched the glass. He wanted to let Bev know he cared, but he didn't want to be pushy.

Katie met him at the bottom of the stairs with arms crossed and foot tapping. Then everything became clear. He *wasn't* being pushy. Katie was. "Want me to go along for moral support?"

"I'll leave that door open. You decide."

"The day has been tough. I wouldn't mind seeing Bev again."

Kevin picked a stack of documents up from the table and stuffed them into his black leather briefcase, wondering what Katie meant. "You're welcome to come, but Bev won't have time to spend with either of us. If you come, it's simply to accompany me and be at the meeting."

"We'll see about that. I'm sure Bev would take time to talk to me."

Kevin zipped the case shut and motioned to the dining room table, disappointed in himself that he hadn't caught on sooner. "Do you need to sit and talk?"

"Why?"

"You're dropping a lot of clues into our conversation."

Katie pulled out a chair and sat at the dark walnut dining table her grandmother had given to her mother. "You know me pretty well, don't you? Mom called today."

Kevin sat adjacent to her. "She did? She hasn't called for a week. How is she doing?"

"Well, she said the hotel is noisy, people at the research center are pushy, and information is hard to come by. She said a lot of the stuff she's looking for has seemed to disappear."

Was he so dense that he didn't understand what Jenny had meant when she said she'd be back *after* she was finished? Didn't he get the clue when she left Katie in his charge? Didn't her very body language indicate she had already dismissed her father and daughter from her mind in her quest to get her "research" done? Kevin sensed Katie's abandonment. "Did she want to know how we're doing?"

"No…she didn't ask." Katie hung her head then lifted it just as quickly and furrowed her brows. "We both know Mom is really into this. Sometimes I think she just can't help herself. I mean, if you were married to my dad and he treated you the way he did us all those years, how would you act? I think she just needs something to occupy her time. This is the way she copes."

Kevin blinked with surprise. "Katie, how did you get to be so mature? I would think you'd want your mom to feel that being here is more important than anything else she's doing."

"You're already here for me."

Kevin hung his head for a moment then stared with pride. "Thanks, honey. Do you know what kind of research she's doing?"

"No, Gramps. I think she would have told us if she wanted us to know. Maybe she's involved with some secret organization and has to keep everything confidential."

He chuckled. He'd let Katie have her opinions about her mother, for now. However, if Jenny didn't see fit to come home soon, he'd find out why. "Okay, Katie, we won't talk about Mom's adventure right now, but I have something I do need to talk about. You think you could help me do something?"

"Sure. What is it?"

"Hattie traveled back over to her motel room in Pensacola to repack then headed somewhere else for a few days. I need to contact her to see if she has any decorating plans drawn up for the diner."

Katie's mouth dropped open. "The diner is so unique. Are you sure you want to change it? The diner is the fifties right down to the marbled design in the gray linoleum. Did you see that jukebox? I love the diner, Gramps. I wouldn't change a thing."

"I understand, but customers your age don't bring in the business. We need to please the eye of those who frequent the place. When you get a chance, call Hattie for me. Her number is stuck with a red thumbtack to the corkboard near the phone. She's given me some fantastic input so far, Katie. Work with me on this."

She let out a long moan. "Okay. At least I'll keep busy while you're gone tonight. You promise nothing is going on between you two? Hattie's kind of a flirt."

"She's a huge flirt, but she doesn't turn my head. Set the alarm after I leave, and don't go anywhere."

"Promise I will set it, but when are you going to let me get a car so I can go out on my own?"

He patted her on the forearm. "When you get a job so you can pay for the car."

"Got your phone with you?"

"Yes, are you going to call me?"

"You need to call me so I don't worry. I predict that you and Bev will be going out together after the meeting, and I want you to let me know."

* * *

"How'd you get so lucky to find out about the sale, Bev, before we did?" Max poured club soda on the griddle before he turned it off, bringing the bubbling mixture to a chocolate-brown color as it lifted the grease.

Bev handed him a pair of clear plastic goggles. "Here, I ran these through the dishwasher last night. Don't forget to use them before you start running your brass brush across the griddle to clean it. Remember last week, how you got a spot of the gunk in your eye?"

Max positioned the goggles over his eyes. "Yeah, I won't quickly forget my trip to the emergency room."

"In answer to your question, I found out about the sale because of my little buddy, the alligator who used to come calling when he got bored at the lake."

Nora brought in the final bin full of dirty dishes to put through the dishwasher. "You really need to call animal control and get that gator out of the park. You know the conservation officer has been pulling every stray gator he can from the lake."

Max lifted his goggles and directed his attention to Bev. "My question still doesn't have an answer."

Bev moved the goggles back over Max's eyes and stared at him face to face. "The owner of the diner showed up in my mobile home park. He came to the rescue when he found out I had the gator for a visitor. We just talked, that's all."

Max shrugged. "Oh."

"I called the CO after Kevin caught the gator. I don't think it'll be a problem anymore." Bev headed into the restaurant's dining room where Esther and Judy had pushed three tables together. They'd put clean coffee cups and saucers at each place and removed all the condiments except for the creamers and sugar from each table. Her gaze shifted to the windows that stretched clear across the front, searching for any sign that Kevin was coming.

"Don't worry," said Esther. "He'll be here soon."

"Do you know him very well?" asked Judy. "Will he be fair with us?"

Bev walked back to the table. "I don't know him *real* well, but I believe he'll be fair. We just have to listen to what he has to say. Everything to do with the diner will all work out. I'm sure of it."

Just then, a set of lights penetrated into the restaurant as Kevin parked his van in front of the building. Esther slipped back through to the kitchen while Judy pulled out a chair and sat down. Kevin turned off his lights and sat in his van for a short time, giving all the employees time to come out and sit down.

After a short period, he got out of the van with a briefcase under his arm and his cell phone in his hand. Looking relaxed in his jeans and sports shirt, Bev was sure he wanted to appear friendly and not like a haughty businessman. As she opened the door for him, she wondered what kind of terms he'd settled on for each of the employees. She tried to appear calm as she leaned against the door and waited for him to enter.

Kevin showed the poise of worldly experience with his smile as he took the door and motioned for her to go in. "Are they ready for me?"

Bev motioned to the back of the restaurant. "I think so. They're a little nervous."

"Thank you, Bev. Good to see you again. Can we talk after the meeting?"

"I'd like that."

"Shall we head back?" He waved his hand in the air to the others.

Bev took in a preparatory breath while she closed the door and locked it then traipsed along behind him. "Is Katie feeling better?"

He continued to focus on the group at the table, offering them his best smile. "Yes, she's fine."

Bev caught up to him in order to make introductions. "Everyone, I'd like you to meet Kevin...I don't know your last name."

He nodded to everyone, all of whom returned his huge smile. "My name is Kevin Sample, but I want you all to feel at home with me. Last names are too formal, so please call me Kevin." He pulled out a chair for Bev to sit down, and he took a spot standing at the head of the table.

Bev squeezed her hands together and rested them in her lap. Esther sat at the opposite end of the table from Kevin. While Bev had remained hopeful about the meeting, she continued to be anxious and stared straight at Kevin, never blinking an eye. Judy sat to her left with arms crossed and teeth digging into her bottom lip. Max and Nora sat together opposite Bev and appeared to be calmer than anyone else.

As Kevin pulled some papers from his briefcase, Max pushed away from the table and headed over to shake his hand. "Max Jenkins. I've been here for as long as I can remember. Started out shucking oysters down at the Gulf and ended up here one day being hired as the cook."

Kevin gave Max's hand a hardy shake. "Max, Bev tells me you're the best cook this side of the Mississippi. I have every intention of keeping you on. You're a good man. I hope you hadn't had any intentions on leaving the diner."

"No sir, I plan on staying on. Thank you." With a relieved look, Max sat back down.

Pleasantly surprised by Kevin's apparent change of heart, Bev knew she could relax. Their fears dwindled to nothing as Kevin in his nonconfrontational blues continued to reassure everyone he had bought the business for only one reason. He was an investor, and he wanted to bring change, but he would never do it at the cost of anyone's job. She could live with a compromise, and another little part of her heart opened for him.

Chapter 8

"Good night, all. See you in the morning," Nora pointed her finger at Kevin. "Now, Mr. Kevin, you feel free to come by anytime, and I'll cook you up that western omelet with hot sauce I told you about tonight."

Kevin walked her to the door and opened it. "Nora, you have a deal. My granddaughter is partial to all those peppers and onions and whatever else you put in one of those things, and I know she'll want to be here with me when you fix it."

Nora gave him a nod as she headed out. "Thanks. I'll see you soon. And thanks for the informative meeting."

Kevin returned the nod. "You drive carefully on those roads, now."

"Bev, you go ahead and get out of here," said Max. "You've been here longer than I have today." Max gathered up all the coffee cups and headed for the kitchen.

She watched for Kevin's reaction. "I agree, Max. I'm

ready to call it a day." She went to the locker to get her purse then walked back across the restaurant.

Kevin gave a thumbs-up to Max and opened the door for Bev. He meandered out behind her. "I have to say, you work with a nice bunch of people in the diner." As the door clicked behind him, he took her arm and assisted her down the steps.

"I'd also have to say they're smitten with you, Kevin. I think you've just won yourself a few friends here in Lake Serenade."

"Would you care to go somewhere and talk?"

Yes, she wanted to go somewhere and talk. "We could sit on the diner's park bench near the pines and magnolia tree. I don't know how much conversation I have in me, to be honest. I'm bushed after the stress of waiting for the meeting to come and go."

"I'd love to sit out here. I'm looking forward to settling this bag of bones for a spell, myself. I stewed all last night and today over this meeting. Once I gave in to do what I knew was right for everyone concerned I was fine, but wrestling with my decisions all day has left me more tired than I want to admit."

"I know you made a great impression on everyone." *Including me.*

He slowly released his hand and removed his phone from his pocket. "Will you excuse me while I call Katie? She had a preconceived notion that I wouldn't come home right after the meeting. She asked me to call her and let her know I'd be late."

"We women have a second sense about some things. I'll just drop here. Tell her I said hello."

Bev brushed off the fragrant pine needles and final magnolia blooms that had fallen onto the bench after the last storm and sat down, enjoying the tepid breeze bringing in a slight salt-sea aroma. She glanced at Kevin. He'd made an impression on her even though he habitually held a part of himself in reserve. He reminded her of a book that stayed open only when someone turned a page and held it there.

To add to the pleasantry, she had connected emotionally with a man who thought his relationships so important that he stayed in touch with his granddaughter so she wouldn't worry.

Had he always been a family man? Huff had been the same type of man, devoted to his parents, nieces, and nephews. Disappointed she had never given him a son or daughter, she pushed the remorse to the back of her mind, glad she'd be able to spend time with Katie.

Before long, Kevin told Katie good-bye and stuck the phone back in his pocket.

"Is she okay with you being late, Kevin?"

"Okay with it?" The bench jostled as he landed. "She wants me to stay out later, but I convinced her you and I weren't inclined to watch the night turn into morning—at least, not tonight."

She gave his comment a moment to soak in then slowly rotated her face toward his. "Are you insinuating we will do so on another night?"

Kevin leaned close and reached his fingers to her temple, where he snatched a small leaf from her hair and dropped it to the ground. "I'm not really a night owl, but I'd like to take you out somewhere nice for dinner. Would you go?"

"I would, Kevin. Would you mind if Katie goes with us? I just can't forget the disappointment in her face yesterday. I think she'd enjoy getting out, especially since her mother's gone."

He stretched his arm across the back of the bench.

"I know for a fact Katie would never turn down the opportunity to go somewhere with you, but I'd like the two of us to go. Would that be okay? A restaurant called Lighthouse Seafood used to be down on the bay. Is it still in business?"

"Oh no, the Lighthouse closed a long time ago. The owners were run out of business by a group who came in from Texas. They have a bunch of restaurants in Florida. They made the family an offer they couldn't refuse. It's always crowded, but the atmosphere doesn't have the personal family touch like most places around here do. And, in answer to your question, I'd like to go with you."

He adjusted his position to look at her. "Will you pick a place and let me know which one?"

"I will."

"I'll call you in a few days, and we'll finalize our plans."

She nodded and looked sidelong up into his eyes. "I'm looking forward to going."

"So am I." He moved his arm and took her hand. "Let's call it a night."

As they stood together, Bev thought about how nicely Kevin networked with everyone. She loved being in his company and hoped the fact he was now her boss wouldn't hinder any personal connection between them. "Thanks for being so kind to everyone. You were a hit."

"Come on, I'll walk you to your car." They walked across the parking lot to her car, and he opened her door. "I'll follow you home."

Bev let go of his hand and got in the car. "There's really no need. I'll be fine."

"No ma'am, I insist. Following you won't take me

much longer. I want to make sure I get you to your door so no one steals you out from underneath me."

He closed her door and got in his van. At this point, she wished the drive were a little longer so she could savor the fact he was behind her, watching over her to make sure she was safe.

Life looked good now and felt good, too, but she didn't really know who he was, and he didn't know her. Then she pushed away the inevitable storms to come for two previously married people spending time together. Facts too personal for her to share now continually prodded at her mind, and only God Himself could give Kevin the grace to accept her sin-stained past.

Kevin had been put on hold on his phone call to one of his companies in New York. The lively baroque music was anything but relaxing, so he thought about more enjoyable things, such as his conversation with Bev last week after the meeting. He'd enjoyed reliving that moment throughout the week. Nevertheless, his current task had him tied up in knots.

Two of his companies in Upper New York State were floundering due to the economy, and he needed to prune back his labor costs. He had no other course of action. Who would be the first to go? At least, being down here in the panhandle, he didn't have to face the people he employed at that company. Nevertheless, he'd become more and more aware of how people counted on him to make all the right choices. Hadn't he just made a good decision in Lake Serenade?

A sudden thought came to him about trusting the God he once knew. He used to until Millie died. *Why didn't God... ?* He stopped the train of thought. *One wasn't supposed to question God, right? One was supposed to trust Him, depend on Him to direct one's life.*

The unsolicited thought further exasperated him until he set his eyes on Katie's study Bible, which was buried at the bottom of her cooking and interior design magazines. He pressed the End button on the phone.

The sun had just begun to peek through the grove across the street, and Katie wouldn't be up for a couple hours. He looked in the direction of the stairs while he extricated the faded blue leather Bible from its blanket of paper. He'd put it back before she stirred from her sleep.

When he thought about this lifeline to the God he once knew intimately, he remembered all about God's love and His forgiveness. He knew God would take him back the moment he asked. Yet something hindered him from opening the Bible and reading it. He knew exactly where to go for comfort, but he couldn't open the Bible yet. His gaze switched to the phone. He had to make the call.

Returning the Bible to its place, Kevin organized his thoughts then picked up the phone. After he dialed in Zane Courtland's number, he headed out the front door to the old rocker on the front porch. One of the few items remaining from Millie's collection of antiques, it had been in her family for generations and had occupied a visible spot in all their homes. As he settled into the chair, his call went through. "Zane Courtland here."

"Zane, buddy. This is Kevin Sample. How's it going up in New York?"

"You must have gotten my e-mail."

Kevin's even heel-toe movement started the sway of the chair, one rocker continually hanging up in the wedge created where one wood porch slat lay lower than the others. "I got your e-mail two days ago, Zane. I've been trying to figure out how to work things. I may need to come up and straighten things out."

The voice at the other end faltered. "Straighten what out? I simply wanted to let you know about production. Sales are down a little, that's all. I'm sure things will pick up once the end of summer comes. We don't need any straightening."

Kevin shifted the chair to a smoother section of porch then sat back down. "I'm not sure we can wait until then. Do you have a feel for who is expendable in the company?"

"Now wait a minute, boss. I'm not sure you got the drift of what I was saying. I'm not asking you to fire anyone. I just wanted to apprise you of—"

"No, you wait a minute." Kevin balked at the voice inside his head as he pumped his rocker harder. *"Trust Me, Kevin."*

Why should God be moving in on him at this point in his conversation? He could do fine on his own. Kevin had done this so many times before. Didn't firing people come under the concept of pruning so more fruit could grow? *Who am I kidding? I've got to get a grip on my life.*

"Kevin, I'd like you to call me back in a few. We've escalated to a battle of wills here, and I know you don't want us to argue. I know *I* don't want to argue. We've been friends for too long. Can we talk later after we've had time to pray about this?"

Kevin's heels came to rest on the porch. The rocking had been just as edgy as his conversation, one that defined the angst that had been building for weeks. Where was Jenny anyway? Didn't she have the guts to get down here and raise her daughter? What was so important up in Tallahassee that she couldn't break away for one day and come see Katie? Zane's words brought Kevin to the truth—he didn't need to solve his business issues; he needed to solve his family issues. "You're right, Zane. I don't know what got into me. I'll call you in a few days, bud. We can't afford to let this relationship crash."

"Thanks, Kevin. Our business issues will work out—they always do between us."

Everyone Kevin knew talked about God as if He were a next-door neighbor whom you could converse with anytime you wanted when you weren't man enough to find your own answers. Even Millie talked to him—and Katie. Why didn't Jenny? His heart pounded wildly deep within his chest as he worked feverishly to calm himself down.

Before long, the aroma of coffee lured Kevin out of the chair and back into the house. "Morning, Katie."

"Gramps. Here, I poured you a cup. Have you called Bev yet?"

"Haven't had time." A rush of caffeine filled his veins as he chugged the warm coffee down. "We really have to get a new pot. Our current one doesn't even heat the coffee thoroughly."

Katie took a loaf of bread out of the bread keeper and opened it up. After she turned the toast indicator to light brown, she stuck one slice into a slot and pushed on the lever. "Don't change the subject. I thought you had a good time with her the night of the meeting."

"I did, and I was supposed to call her. Anyway, I have a lot of other things going on right now." Kevin poured himself another cup of coffee. "We can talk about something other than Bev."

"This is a golden opportunity. Why don't you see

that? Someone could whisk in and take her away from you."

Kevin laughed as he pulled out a kitchen chair and sat at the table. "Did you get a hold of Hattie for me, Katie?"

She reached for her Bible and pulled out a business card stuck in the middle. "Yep, she answered on the first ring. I called yesterday just to check when she's coming back." She handed him the card. "She has a couple more drawings to work on, and then she'll call us back."

Kevin took the card and slipped it into the top pocket of his red T-shirt. "Wonderful. Thanks."

"So, about Bev. Can we talk?"

"Who's going to take her away?"

"You don't know. Somebody may be waiting for her."

"She doesn't act like she's attached."

"Just because she didn't tell us there was someone, doesn't mean he doesn't exist."

Kevin balked. Katie was quick with the quips—quicker than he was. "This is a small town with few people. No one has come for her, so far. I don't think she's going anywhere, and I don't think anyone else will sweep her away."

"Not even the dollar-sixty-seven man?"

Kevin roared with laughter. "What? Who is the dollar-sixty-seven man?"

After Katie's toast popped up, she got a new jar of fruit spread from the cupboard, popped the lid, and spread a small amount over the surface of the warm bread. "I'm glad you asked. He's been coming into the diner for years. His trademark is the tip he leaves. Nora told me he leaves Bev a tip with a smile—a dollar bill, two quarters, a dime, a nickel, and two pennies, which he places on the bill next to his coffee cup. On his way out, he doesn't wait for anyone to come to the register. He just lays down a tip for her then leaves."

"What a ridiculous way to get someone's attention. I've never heard anything about him." Kevin retrieved a banana from the refrigerator and peeled the skin away. "I'm not worried."

Katie bit off a piece of bread then stuffed the rest in the garbage disposal. "Maybe she doesn't want you to know. Maybe you'd better take notice. He comes every morning, and Nora told me he's been trying to woo Bev for a long time. Possibly you need to stop by there and get involved with your new diner."

Katie disappeared quicker than usual, and a rush of apprehension blasted his gut. Kevin wanted to get together with Bev again. He had just assumed she'd be available whenever he called her. Suddenly, time seemed to run over him like a semi over a Smart Car. He didn't want to hurry, but if he were honest with himself, he didn't want to lose her either. His face twisted in a scowl as he checked the time. If he were smart he'd head over to the diner—after he stopped at the florist.

Chapter 9

"What's this I hear about you and the New Yorker?" Sam Talisman wiped his mouth with the paper napkin, crumpled it up, and then dropped it on the plate he'd just emptied of two pieces of jelly toast. Without taking his eyes off Bev, he tipped the coffee cup to get the last drink.

Bev was past blushing with Sam. She had explained her reluctance to him so many times she was like a big sister trying to get her insistent little brother to realize apples didn't grow on a pear tree. "Sam, you need to drop this thing you have for me. You and I have nothing in common—with the exception we like to talk. Nothing exists between me and any man from New York."

"What was his name again? Kevin?" He eased off the green plastic bar stool and tugged at the overstuffed billfold he kept in his right back pocket of his cargo pants. "Used to know a man named Kevin who left town in a hurry and traveled up to New York. Could be the same one."

Bev scribbled the cost of his meal and set the guest check down next to his plate. She wasn't going to allow Sam to create any angst in her heart over Kevin. "I don't know what you've been hearing, but Kevin is the new owner of the diner. He met with all of us last week to discuss the diner's future. For your information, I already know he once lived here and left for New York. Your news is not news."

Sam slipped a dollar bill on top of the check and sixty-seven cents on top of the bill before he headed to the register. "Did he discuss his past, too? I have my suspicions about this man."

Bev followed him to the cash register, leaving his check next to his coffee cup. "That'll be five dollars today."

Sam pulled a ten from his wallet, held the bill out to her, and then worked the wallet back into his pants pocket. "Here you go. You know the breakfast costs more than five."

As Bev tried to take it, he held fast. When he winked at her, she couldn't help but smile. They'd reenacted this same scenario at least fifty times over the last year. As Sam's eyes latched onto hers, Kevin walked in the front door.

Bev no longer cared that Sam continued his habitual teasing because, as far as she was concerned, he had just disappeared from view. All she noticed now was Kevin, in his light blue polo shirt and unshaven face, grasping a bunch of pink roses. Captivated with his dimpled smile, Bev let go of the ten, and so did Sam. As Kevin walked toward them, the bill floated to the floor and landed at Kevin's feet. "What do we have here?" He bent to pick the ten up.

Sam, his face inscribed with a touch of jealousy, pressed his thumb and index finger on the ten-dollar bill and removed it from Kevin's hand. "I believe that's mine."

Kevin let go, smiled, and reached out his hand to shake Sam's. "Kevin Sample. Please, allow me to pay for your morning meal. It's on the house."

Sam backed a few steps. "Oh, you're the new owner here. I believe I recognize your name, Mr. Sample. Just so you're aware of who I am, Tom and I go back a number of years. I hope you realize most folks around here feel no one can take Tom's place."

Bev cleared her throat. "Kevin, this is Sam Talisman. We've known each other since high school."

Sam laid his ten on the counter and proceeded out the door. Bev held her breath while she waited for Kevin to respond. "Nice man," he said.

She released the laugh she'd held from the time the money had fallen to the floor. "Don't think anything of the situation. Sam's come around here for ages. He thinks he owns everyone."

"I'm told I need to watch out for him. In fact, I elected to go hungry this morning in order to hurry over here and make sure you were still available." He handed her the roses. "Here, these are for you."

"How beautiful." Bev looked around at the customers whose attention she and Kevin had drawn as she took the roses. "Let me go find a vase in the kitchen." Within a few minutes, she returned holding a transparent green container with six roses arranged with baby's breath. She set them on the counter near the cash register.

"Why don't I help clear some of these tables?"

She pointed to the counter. "A plastic bin is always positioned under the counter, if you want to get it."

Kevin found the bin and then followed Bev around the diner while she placed the dishes into the container. "What brings you in here today?"

"My granddaughter told me about Sam. She has this high degree of respect for you, and you have captured the attention she once gave to me."

Bev wiped the back of her hand across her forehead and stopped to look him in the eye. "Is that so? I'm so flattered. What did she say?"

Kevin glanced over to the kitchen door and lowered his voice. "According to Katie, Nora told her this wild story about Sam wanting you for his own. You and Nora will have to have a talk and clear this up."

Bev walked to the next table and began stacking the plates. "I'll do nothing of the sort. I'm staying out of this one, and you should, too." She teased him with a wink and set the dishes in the bin. "We'd better take this to the kitchen before it gets any fuller."

Bev hadn't even thought about a new man entering her life, but she loved the thought. Should she forget this flutter of foolishness she felt in her heart when Kevin was near? Was he simply teasing her about Sam, or did he mean something by it? She swung open the door. "There you go."

He stationed his foot at the bottom of the door. "You go ahead, I'm right behind you."

She turned and took hold of the bin. "Shall I take these now?"

"No, just show me where to put them."

She pointed at the dishwasher that resembled a miniature Quonset hut with a handle on the top. "If you don't mind, just put them next to the washer, and I'll stack them inside."

"Why don't you show me, and I'll stack them."

A whoosh of steam shot up into Kevin's face as Bev lifted the door. His smile disappeared as he teased. "Towel, please." Nora was standing a few feet away and tossed a dishtowel at him.

"First, we have to unload these and stack them in the shelves near the griddle." Bev turned to point to the cupboards and found the remainder of the staff muffling their laughter.

Judy chuckled. "Don't mind us. We're just enjoying the show." Judy stripped her apron, walked over to Kevin, and held it by the straps for him to put on.

Not to be outdone by anyone's sense of humor, Kevin donned the apron, did a pirouette, and then slouched into a modeling pose before he turned back to the dishwasher. "I think I'm going to like working here."

I'm going to love having you here. Bev piled the dishes to the side as he unloaded the contraption then handed him the dish soap and pointed to the dispenser.

He loaded the dirty dishes inside, pushed the Start button, and then lifted the bottom of the apron to wipe his brow. "Did I do good?"

By now, everyone was in stitches, including Bev. She carried some of the dishes over to the counter. "I think I'll turn this job over to Kevin—he does it so well."

Nora opened the cupboard door. "I could do more, but I'll leave this mess to you all, then. I'm headed home for the day."

Max turned off the griddle, removed his apron, and laid it on the counter next to the grill. "I'm headed back in to cook tonight for that wedding party."

"Oh no," said Bev. "I had forgotten. Do I need to come back?"

Max got his truck keys from the locker and waved her off. "Nothing doing. I got my two teenage daughters and Ina helping me tonight. I'll wait out in front of the diner until they get here to make preparations. You're off the hook."

As Max left, Kevin brought the remainder of the dishes over to the cupboard. He handed each glass to Bev as she stacked them inside the cupboards. "I owe you," she said without looking at him. Then, without thinking, she turned to him and dashed out an invitation. "How about I take you and Katie out to dinner tonight? I know a good shrimp place about thirty miles down the road toward Panama Beach."

"You may, if you allow me to drive. Are you sure you don't want the two of us to go alone?"

"We will, next time."

"Okay, I'll go home and round up my granddaughter, and then we'll come pick you up close to five, okay?"

"Oh, we won't get in anywhere on a Friday night in August if we wait till five. With summer vacation in full swing, we'd have to leave my drive no later than four thirty. If you don't mind, be at my place around three forty-five."

Kevin leaned back on the counter, chuckled, and pointed to the clock on the opposite wall. "That would mean I'd have to turn the clock back by about thirty minutes to get me home and back to you in time."

"Oh. I didn't realize it was so late. What are we going to do?"

"Pizza?"

"Pizza sounds great." She pointed to his apron. "Shall I take your apron?"

"What? You mean you don't like to see me dressed to the hilt?" He loosened the strings and handed it to her.

"You're teasing, right?"

"I am. Do you have any of that delicious sun tea you made the other night?"

Bev pulled off her own apron and dumped both in the dirty clothes container on the other side of the dishwasher. "I make a couple quarts every day this time of year."

He took his cell phone from his pocket. "Why don't I phone in the pizzas, go get Katie, and we'll be back to your place within the hour? Anthony's pizza place okay?"

She worried she wasn't worthy of him. But if she couldn't forgive herself, how could he forgive her? "That sounds great! I'll see you when you get to my place."

Kevin took her hand. "You hesitated. Would you prefer not to do this tonight? We can make plans another time."

They locked gazes as his warm hand cradled hers. "Not at all. I mean, yes, I want to do this tonight. I had my mind on something else and...anyway, yes, let's get pizza, and I'll see you at my place in a little while. I can't wait to see Katie again."

He didn't speak for a short time as he stared into her eyes, but his smile said everything she wanted to hear. She hoped her smile did the same for him. He took in a deep breath then exhaled. "I guess we'd better go, if we're going to make our date on time." He squeezed her hand before he let go then started for the door.

Their relationship was going so well that right now wasn't the time to ruin anything by revealing past mistakes. Right now was the time to get to know each other and build a solid foundation. They'd talk about everything eventually. Nothing could touch them before then.

"I won't go without you, Katie, and I won't say any more on the subject. I want you to go to Bev's house with me, and so does Bev." Kevin slipped a light-yellow sweater over a beige-and-blue plaid shirt. "Should I wear socks with these khakis?"

"Back up a little bit, and let me see." Katie gave him a once over. "You look great, but I suggest you wear some socks since you're wearing your moccasins. If you wear your beach sandals, you could get by without socks." Katie snatched her sweater from the back of a dining room chair. "Now, I really think you could get so much more accomplished if you went alone."

"So many choices." Kevin walked into the laundry room and rummaged through the basket of clean clothes. He emerged with a dark-brown pair of socks. "She suggested you come."

"Maybe she's only being nice, but based on the fact you're showing a little promise, I'll go with you this one time. Do I need to bring a book to read so you can at least be alone on the porch while I read in the living room?"

Kevin searched through the bits of paper Katie was prone to use for telephone messages. "Did Hattie return my call?"

"Oh, I forgot to tell you. She called and is anxious to meet with you to get something set up. She flew out to a job in Wisconsin and should be back in a day or so. She said something about visiting a man named Ted down on Anna Maria Island when she's done here."

"Hmm. I hope she has time to work with me on decorating the diner." Kevin pointed at the door. "Go. I'm right behind you." He set the alarm and followed Katie into the sultry night air. His life had taken a surprising turn these last few months. From the time he had secretly visited the diner during Christmas and made his decision to purchase it, he'd had Bev Lahmeyer in the back of his mind.

He couldn't say Bev was the reason he'd bought the diner, but he could say he had looked forward to meeting her. He could say, with certainty, Bev was quickly edging her way into his heart.

While he agonized over Jenny's reason for staying away so long, in this situation he was glad. Things might not progress at all if Jenny were home. Having been the only child, Jenny would more than likely make a scene if she knew her father had fallen for someone besides her mother.

Chapter 10

"Bev, this is Jack Kindler."

"Jack. We haven't talked for eons. I'd thought you'd retired by now. To what do I owe this phone call?" Bev hugged the landline phone between her ear and shoulder as she headed outside to the front of the lanai. She snatched up the jar of sun tea from the grass, brushed away the loose clippings, and walked back inside.

"Bev, I thought you might want to know. My assistant, Alicia, came into the law office this morning to find the files had been ransacked. The entire contents of my file drawers were strewn about the floor. She called the police immediately and then went through the files. Some things were missing. She was pretty familiar with most of them and has re-filed the bulk of the mess."

Bev let out a moan with the whoosh of the lanai door closing behind her. She had a feeling Jack wasn't telling her the whole story. "Oh no, you're kidding me."

"I know this is upsetting, but we're trying to do everything we can. I felt you should know." Jack had that annoying tone in his voice she remembered from years past. Nevertheless, Bev had chosen him based on referrals and his excellent track record.

She'd made the decision to allow him to handle her legal affairs over forty years previously. Why did the rashness of her immature decisions in the seventies still pinch as if they took place yesterday? "Don't tell me this actually happened."

"I'm sure your files are simply scattered here on the floor with the rest. Alicia has been able to match up most of the paperwork with each of the files it was dumped out of. I just wanted to let you know about the break-in."

"That's not good enough, Jack. You told me you were entering all my information into your computer so no paper trail would follow. I can't afford to have my information compromised in any way." Bev wandered into the kitchen and set the jar on the counter. "Let me know as soon as you have anything else on this."

"I'm sorry, Bev. I've tried to break this gently, but if I were totally honest, it doesn't look good. As we speak, Alicia is gathering the last of the papers from the floor. She's shaking her head at me. I'm afraid they're gone."

"Find them, Jack. I don't care what it takes. Find my paperwork." Bev bit back the tears forming in her eyes as she hung up the phone. She had put this all behind her. She had let go of all the blunders she had made and gave her life to God. A new start. That's what Pastor Canon had told her. This would be a fresh start. He told her not to ever look back but to look forward to what God had in store for her. Why hadn't she ever been able to quit looking back?

When she told Huff about her past, he brushed it off as though it were a piece of lint on a fine garment. He didn't care what had happened before. He only cared about what God had for their future. Then, he died. He died and left her alone to face this mess.

The timing wasn't fair. *Lord, I know You've been with me this far. I know I'll have to tell Kevin sooner or later, but I'm not ready yet. Whoever has stolen those papers that reveal my past life, please let their purposes come to nothing. Please, give me a reprieve and let me live my life under Your forgiveness.*

Bev headed for the bathroom, closed the door behind her, and took three deep breaths while she turned on the cold water faucet. Kevin would be coming soon, and she didn't want a red swollen face from crying. As soon as the water ran cold, she let it run over her hands and her wrists then splashed some on her face a few times. "Oh God, help me. I can't fall apart now. This night is too important to me. Help me through every moment, and give me the grace to live each day after."

She pulled a hand towel from the rod and headed back out to the living room, drying her face and eyes. When she looked out the window, Kevin's van headed toward her home. The last traces of the beautiful warm day evident in the blazing orange ball in the distant west seemed to shout hope to her, but she wasn't sure any hope remained.

She took in another deep breath, laying the towel across the back of a dining room chair, as the van pulled into her drive. *Put your past behind you.*

Katie was out of the van about the time Bev got to the door. Bev swung the door wide open and put on a smile. "Katie, welcome. The pizza smells so good."

The floral fragrance of the lanai vanished, replaced

by a spicy aroma of Italian cuisine when Katie, her arms laden with three pizza boxes, stepped inside. "Thanks. Should I put these in the kitchen?"

Bev held the door for Kevin and motioned him in. "Sure, you know the way." She focused on Kevin, hoping he couldn't see past the smile on her face.

Kevin stopped short of walking in the door. "May I enter also? I know I'm not the one with the food, but if I beg, may I come in as well?"

"Don't do it!" Katie had edged up on Bev and stood next to her in the doorway. "I don't know who this man is, and if he doesn't get up enough nerve to take you on a date—alone—I'll totally disown him."

Kevin looked to his right and his left and shrugged his shoulders. He looked much like a little boy who had lost his way. "I am more than willing to take this stunning woman on a date alone."

Unable to answer his bold comment, she backed away from the door. "In that case, you may come in." She waved a hand toward the kitchen. "I believe our meal awaits, and the smell is driving me mad. Let's eat!"

Kevin's kind words dulled her pain. He followed Katie into the kitchen, and Bev brought up the rear. She'd try to put the entire gloom of today behind her and hope for the best. He'd know all about her soon enough.

Jack would find the person who had stolen her file. He was one of the best attorneys around. He'd put the best investigators on the case. If he didn't figure out what happened, Bev's private life would be public knowledge, and the pain and embarrassment would prove to be more than she could handle.

* * *

"I don't want to hear any more about you not wanting to get out of the house. You two have been so busy; you haven't taken any time for yourselves. I've got the cleanup handled." Katie stood in front of the kitchen sink and stretched her arms out like a crossing guard.

Kevin extended his hand to Bev. "She means business. Shall we?"

Bev shrugged. "We don't have a choice."

Kevin clasped her hand in his as they headed out of the lanai and down the street to the lake. "I'm almost jealous you have such a beautiful view out here."

Bev held securely to his hand. "I've loved living here. My husband and I had an apartment, for a while, down near the Gulf but found the threat of hurricanes more than enough to move us inland. I'm close enough to enjoy the coast yet far enough away to be able to evacuate quickly, if need be."

"I remember living with the threat, but I can't imagine that this span of land has ever been under threat of being washed away. You sit so high."

"I know, Kevin, but storms do happen. I'm in a prime area and constantly live with the risk, but I try to leave all the results in God's hands."

Bev waved to Helen and Robert, who were sitting outside on their deck.

"He's the man who was here after the gator, right?"

Bev nodded. "I feel so sorry for them. They both have a long road ahead."

Kevin waved also. "I have a feeling you'll be helping them out."

As they walked a little further, Bev waved to another woman and a man who lived across the street from the woman. "They've got a *thing* going on."

Kevin chuckled. "A lot goes on around here, doesn't it? You do keep close track of everyone."

"Does my concern show? I've never wanted to be one of those loners who has nothing to do but spy on her neighbors. Even so, word gets around in a small community like this one."

"Do you suppose they're talking about us?" He gave her hand a gentle squeeze.

She smiled and shook her head. "I don't doubt they are."

Even though he'd purchased this mobile home park a long time ago, he didn't want this lifestyle. He had dreams of getting away from places such as this and owning his own home on a few acres of land. Nonetheless, his mellow mood when he was with Bev had him thinking he might give in to the urge to change his life around and live wherever she lived.

He might even turn his life around. Millie had insisted on it when he was married to her, and Bev deserved having a husband to lead her spiritually. But that was easier said than done. "What made you buy here in the first place?"

"Necessity."

"Necessity?"

"We moved here when we were both in our forties. We'd spent our nest egg on setting Huff up in his own garden shop. Once we got his business paid off, we tried to stash some money aside for another home. He knew the man who managed the park, and he let us move here before we were eligible. The guy understood we had no children and no plans to have them, so he trusted us to behave, I guess."

"So you started watching over these folks a long time ago."

Bev laughed. "I guess when I look at my situation from your viewpoint, we do watch over one another. At least we all keep one another in line."

He pointed to the brilliant colors in the west. "Look at the sunset."

"Every sunset is new. Do you want to wait and watch the colors evolve or just keep walking around the mobile home park? Eventually the road circles back around."

"I thought of suggesting that myself."

"No you didn't. You're teasing me."

Kevin loosened his hand from hers and rested his arm around her shoulder as dusk moved in. Intoxicated by the sunset, the warmth of the still night air, being next to the loveliest woman he had met in years, he whispered Bev's name then pressed his lips to her cheek in a delicate but measured effort to let her know he cared.

Bev slipped her arm around his waist. "I never thought I'd feel this way again, Kevin."

He wanted to stop and pull her closer, look her in the eyes and promise to do right by her. He wanted to say to her all the things that would make her feel secure and wanted, but he continued on around the road simply enjoying her closeness.

Millie hadn't warmed up to him very quickly. He recalled the first peek at his young bride as she rounded the corner in the Wayland Methodist Church and began her walk down the aisle on her father's arm. She hadn't allowed him to kiss her, yet and waiting for her first kiss at the altar was electrifying.

He glanced over at Bev walking beside him. She had her head turned west, watching the same unforgettable sun he and Millie had watched from the beach in Hawaii when they were on their honeymoon. Those days were past, and he couldn't help but remember standing with his hand on her casket as the same people who came to their wedding paraded by and offered their condolences at the loss of his precious wife.

He focused his attention ahead while the cicadas' prolonged buzz gave way to the crickets' song. Being with Bev now, feeling the gradual waning of his longing for Millie, and Katie's insistence he give Bev a chance—all played a part to make this moment special and right. He nuzzled his face into her hair and delicately pressed his lips against it, and she cuddled closer to him.

Before long the sun settled into the horizon reflecting different hues of fuchsias and lilacs like shimmering gems into iridescent Lake Serenade. Bev pointed to their left. "I think God saved the most beautiful one for tonight, don't you?"

He stopped and turned to her. "I'm looking at the most beautiful one right now."

She peered up into his face with a dreamlike smile. "I can't remember the last time anyone smothered me with sweetness."

He stroked his hand through her hair. "I hope more chances are in the offing."

"I believe those chances are good."

He could have lingered for hours, but he found himself continually trying to pace himself with the romance thing. "Shall we head back?"

She smiled and took his hand. "We're rounding the circle, Kevin. Give it some time, and we'll be heading back west again."

Kevin smiled back, enjoying the warmth of her hand. "Maybe I do belong in an old folk's trailer park."

"I know you're teasing me, but don't ever call this

an old folk's park around any of the residents. It's an *over-fifty* mobile home park."

"I am having fun at your expense. Please, forgive me. Shall we change the subject?"

"Okay. Tell me about Jenny. Is Katie a lot like her?"

Yes, she and Katie were much alike, but Katie had more of a genuine compassion for people. Jenny was more abrupt and to the point, perhaps because of what she had gone through in her life. He didn't blame her for the time she rebelled against him and Millie when she was a teenager. She had a right to, based on the family dynamic. "In some ways Katie is unique."

Bev froze in her tracks just as a cool flash of air from the woods encircled them. "Stop, Kevin." She pointed straight ahead of them. "Look over near the marsh… those eyes peeking out of the settlings. Suppose it could be another gator?"

"I think you might be right. Come on." They continued cautiously past the area. "The eyes are close together. Could be. It can't be the one who ended up in your shed though. He's at the zoo. I'm trying to figure out how another one wandered into this area."

"I don't want to linger." She tugged his hand as she moved on around the circle. "The conservation officer said he thought our friend was a stray. People around here have been known to give up their exotic pets to any body of water they can find. When I got home from work the other day, I noticed the conservation team was here again. I stopped to see what they were doing, and they said they'd been trying to trap two more gators. They put up a no swimming sign for the time being."

Kevin and Bev strolled along the circular road back to her place. Holding hands with this captivating woman had made the evening perfect. Neither spoke the remainder of the way. At her lanai door, she turned to him, and Kevin touched his fingertips to her temple as if touching fine silk then let them drift downward over her cheek as he whispered, "I didn't know I'd enjoy this evening so much."

She pressed her hand against the top of his hand and let her fingers slide across it as she lifted her face toward his. Then his lips caressed hers briefly before she pulled away. She smiled, and he took both her hands in his. Surely nothing could ruin this night.

Katie ran out onto the lanai and opened the door with Kevin's cell phone at her ear. "Gramps, we've got a problem. Mom's on the phone. She's in jail. She wants to know if you can come up to Mundy right away."

Kevin reached for the phone as Katie ran back inside and fell into a chair in tears. He followed her in. "Jenny? Hello, Jenny?" He lowered the phone and pushed the End button. "That's strange. She didn't answer."

Bev followed Kevin inside and positioned the other chair next to Katie and put her arm around her shoulder. "Katie, what happened?"

Katie wiped a tear that had rolled down her cheek and shook her head. "She was making her one phone call, and she talked kinda fast. I got the impression she didn't have much time to talk. How could she be in jail?"

Kevin lowered himself to the floor to sit. He rested his hand on Katie's and stared at Bev in amazement. "Do they put you in jail because of traffic tickets? Last I'd heard, she had seven parking tickets and one speeding ticket. Why else could she be in jail?"

Bev shrugged. "Can we trace the call somehow?"

"No, the call was blocked," said Katie.

"Imagine how embarrassed she must have been to have to admit to Katie where she was," said Bev.

"If this arrest had to do with her tickets, she has no one to blame but herself." Kevin stood and began pacing the width of the lanai.

Bev got out of the chair and waved him down after the third turn. "Kevin, please sit down before you drive yourself crazy. Maybe you should just talk this through."

This scenario had to be a bad nightmare. No man ever pictures his precious little girl in jail. He wanted to cry and grieve. This reminded him of all the things she had gone through in her life.

He took the chair next to Katie, and Bev knelt down beside him and took his hand in hers. She stared up into his eyes until he relented and looked into hers. Her smile of empathy riveted into his soul. "God would never abandon us, Kevin, and you can't abandon your only daughter. Can you help her? Katie is welcome to stay here with me for however long you take up there."

Katie looped her arm through Kevin's. "Please, Gramps, Bev's right. I would hate if you didn't go. I need to know what's going on with her. Maybe she's in real trouble and needs help."

"If Jenny called you, she needs you to come," said Bev. "I feel her plea is urgent."

Bev and Katie had their say, and Kevin felt he couldn't turn them down. For a moment, he stared at Bev kneeling beside him and read past her pleading look. He could tell from the expression in her eyes she needed to see him relinquish all to help his daughter. If he neglected to respond to this obligation, his relationship with Bev would suffer. So would his authority over his granddaughter. "What do you think, Katie? Do you want to stay here?"

"Yes, yes, and yes. You head north and take care of Mom. I'd rather be here instead of alone at your place."

Kevin got to his feet then tugged Bev's hand. She stood up next to him, and he folded his arms around her, pulling her close to deaden the pain. Holding her seemed natural and safe.

Then Bev released from his embrace. "I'll take her home tomorrow morning to get some clothes, and she can go into work with me. They won't mind if I'm a little late."

"Thank you, Bev."

"May I do anything for you while you're gone?"

"I only have one thing that needs tending to, depending on how long my trip takes. I can't reschedule my decorator. She already has her flight plans made. Can you and Katie handle talking to her for me?"

Bev glanced at Katie. "If you trust us, we'll handle the meeting."

Katie got up from the chair and put her arms around Kevin. "You go ahead, Gramps, but be careful. Florida roads aren't too safe at night. I'll be fine here with Bev."

Kevin lifted his wallet from his back pocket, found Hattie's card, and handed it to Bev. He swiped his hand across the sweat on his forehead. "You remember Hattie. The number written on the back in pencil is the hotel where she'll be staying in Pensacola, if you can't reach her on her cell." He took out a folded piece of paper and handed it to her. "Here are a few of the ideas she and I talked about. At least my scribbles will give you an idea of the direction I'd like to go."

"Don't worry about missing your meeting with her. We'll arrange something with her."

He extended his arm to Bev. "I wish you could go."

Bev slipped one arm around his waist and walked with him to the door. "You need me here."

He let go and opened the door. "I'll try to give you both a call when I know more." He hadn't felt this numb since Millie had died. He knew the arrest was about more than traffic tickets. Some family dynamic—Carl died in prison, and now Jenny was in jail. What a heritage to leave one's daughter. He swallowed the lump in his throat after he was outside and the door had closed behind him.

Katie stole into the house as Bev walked to the door and stared adoringly at him while they each placed their hands up to the glass to meet one another. If nothing else, he'd seal this night with a nonverbal pledge of faithfulness, trust, and love. He'd begun to realize that's where he was with her: in love.

Chapter 11

Bev shot up out of a sound sleep, struggled to get the covers off, and then swung her feet over the side of the bed. Splatters of water tapped on the window in a syncopated cadence from the outside sprinkler system, but everything else was still. As the moonlight spread a sliver of light down the side of her bed, she bent down to feel underneath for her flip-flops and positioned them so she could slide her feet into them.

Did a shriek awaken her at two o'clock in the morning, or did a nightmare descend on her from her emotional overload? A myriad of possibilities swam in her head from the baby alligator ending up on someone's lanai to Robert's wife, Helen, wandering out into the night and getting lost and even to Katie in the room next to hers.

A click of the air-conditioner and a whoosh of air coming from the vent in the floor sent a patch of goose bumps up her arms and down her back. *You're being silly, Bev. You're hearing things.* Nevertheless, she grabbed her bathrobe, which was tangled up in the heap of blankets at the end of her bed, then turned it right side out. While she put her arms through each sleeve, she made her way across the room to the doorway.

She had kept the door ajar about an inch the night before so she could hear if Katie got up. Drawing the door open enough to see out, she did a quick scan and noticed Katie heading from the kitchen back toward her room. Bev decided to check things out.

After she tied her robe, she roamed into the living room and found Katie wrapped in her jungle-print throw and huddled on the couch. "Katie, I don't want to startle you, but are you okay?"

Katie twisted the corner of the throw in her fist and dabbed it at her eyes. "I thought I could do this quietly. I'm sorry I awakened you."

Bev sat down next to her and put her arm around Katie's shoulders. "I thought I heard a shriek and thought I'd better see what happened. That wasn't you, was it?"

"I'm sorry I woke you."

"I don't want to pry, but I just want to let you know I'm here if you need me. I'm sure this deal with your mother has you upset. I don't know what's going on, but you don't have to be alone in this if you don't want to."

Katie leaned her head on Bev's shoulder. "I guess a hug is all I need right now. I was feeling really lonely and couldn't seem to get a grip on things. The shriek you heard was one of my wild sobs. I probably should have tried staying put in bed and falling asleep."

Bev hadn't had the luxury of talking openly with her mother or grandmother when she was younger. Women didn't do much confiding back then. Today's women tended toward communication. "We women are so unique in our feelings. One minute we're happy, and the next minute, we're sad. In the daytime, we feel we could attack a den of lions, but at night we cower at the shadows. Do you think that will ever change?"

Katie began to cry. "I think if the lions came one at a time, I'd be able to handle them. It's just that I can't seem to recover from one attack before another lion takes me on."

"Sometimes, a person needs another person to come out and slay the lion with you." Bev thought about her own issues. She could speak to Katie from experience. Two lions were standing before her right now—the lion of her past and the lion of her future. Both had her frozen in her tracks.

Katie sat up, pushed the blanket to the floor, and turned on the table lamp behind her. Using the sofa arm as a backrest, she picked up the blanket and spread it across her lap. "Okay, you talked me into sharing. Here's the problem."

Bev turned on the other lamp, drew her feet underneath her, and faced Katie. "I'm all ears."

"I'll turn eighteen at the end of the summer. But Gramps doesn't realize that according to society I'll be a grown woman ready to be out on my own. On the other hand, I'm scared to death. I lost my father, and now I'm losing my mother. I don't know what she's up to." Katie pulled the neckline of her T-shirt up to dab at her eyes. "I've tried to pretend coming of age and being an adult doesn't bother me, but it does."

"And now, this news that has catapulted your grandpa off to see what he can do."

"Yes, and I don't know for sure what's going on." Red-eyed, Katie shook her head and looked at Bev.

"Don't you think I have a right to know what's going on? She could be in trouble, and I wouldn't be able to do a thing to help. Don't you think Gramps should be more forthcoming on whatever is going on? Mom is acting so mysterious."

"I don't know, Katie. Sometimes we adults get so wrapped up in the present we neglect to realize how our lives are affecting those around us. I'd bet your mother doesn't even realize how this is affecting you."

Katie summed up her confusion with a frown. "I told Gramps as much, but I didn't believe my own words. Mom and Dad were already separated when Dad passed on. He hadn't been allowed to see me, and she never went to visit him, as far as I know. Gramps tried to help him, but even he was too late to do any good. My mother shut my dad out of her life a long time ago—because of me."

"No, Katie, because of what he did to you."

"What?" Katie rolled the blanket into a ball and stuffed it into her ribs. "What do you know about that?"

Bev felt a rush of heat to her face as she searched for a way to answer Katie without incriminating Kevin. She stretched her right hand out to Katie and wiggled the first two fingers. "See these? They'll never be normal. I'll always have the pain to remind me."

Katie's mouth dropped open as she took hold of Bev's hand and rubbed her fingers across the crooked fingers with enlarged joints. Tears pooled at her lids as she gave Bev a long searching look. "What happened?"

"I had an abusive father, Katie. I've learned how to read in between the lines when I talk with people from similar backgrounds. The problem back in my day was people didn't talk about abuse. A family member could ravage another under the secrecy of the family unit. Many things from my past were never dealt with, including my father's excessive behavior. My mother would never own up to the fact she knew about his abuse or listen to what I had to say."

"I'm so sorry. I would never imagine you had a problem with abuse."

"I hide my past well. Anyway, I had to learn his abuse wasn't my problem. His abuse was his problem. Still, I loved him and looked at him as my hero. I don't know why. I'm sure he must have loved me in his own way."

Katie sniffed and dabbed her eyes. "I know what you mean. I loved my dad so much, so how could he be so violent to me? How long did the abuse go on for you?"

"All I know is this is when the abuse stopped." Bev held her two fingers in the air and wiggled them back and forth. "I think my father lied about how I had fallen off the back porch. My mother believed him. Nevertheless, when she saw my misaligned fingers, she rushed me to the doctor's office. I'm sure he must have had an idea what happened. I only remember my young mind trying to figure out when I had fallen off the porch and what that had to do with my father pushing me down."

"I'm so sorry, Bev. I know how you feel. Let me show you something." Katie pulled back the long sleeve on her T-shirt then held her forearm out for Bev to see.

Bev ran her fingers across the seven-stitch scar on Katie's wrist. "You didn't, did you?"

Katie pulled her arm back, ran her fingers across the scar, and then pulled her sleeve back down. "No, I didn't attempt suicide. My father pushed me, too. I was holding a tiny crystal angel in my hand. My grandmother had given it to me. I'd heard him and my mother fighting in the entryway of our home. My mom rushed out of the room in tears and ran up the stairs. He came around the corner and saw me crouching under the dining room table with my angel.

"He yanked me up by my arm and pushed me over toward the couch. When he did, my wrist fell under my body while the angel was still wrapped in my hand. Its harp cut into my wrist. My mother rushed me to the hospital and called the police."

A shiver crawled up Bev's back. Katie's revelation had stirred a few of her own memories—complexities of her past that troubled her to this day. "It sounds like your mother did what she had to do. I hope you're not angry with her."

"I'm not. Once she believed me, I felt free to talk to her at the hospital. My mother decided then and there we would leave him. I know he was brokenhearted and maybe even sorry for what he did, but everything after that happened so quickly."

Bev shook her head. "Katie, this calls for a few cups of coffee. Come on to the kitchen and help me. I think you and I are in for a longer conversation than we first thought."

They headed for the kitchen but not before Katie placed her arms around Bev's waist. "You'll never know how much this has meant to me. I guess a lot could be said about being in the right place at the right time."

Bev had heard almost every story a young woman could tell due to working with high school girls in Sunday school. Katie would never know the flood of compassion Bev felt for her. Perhaps, once this arrest issue with Jenny was settled, Kevin would let Bev in on more of this family's background. Nevertheless this scenario seemed different, and it frustrated Bev not to be able to figure out why. Certainly Katie's family's secrets couldn't be any worse than her own.

The sun poured out its light with only the slats in the white wooden shutters on the east window holding the light back. Time hadn't waited for Bev and Katie while they'd devoured two brownies each and finished off a pot of coffee as they talked their hearts out. "Oh my, Katie, look what we've done. I've got to get you home to get some clothes, and then get us both to work."

Katie covered her wide yawn with her hand. "I wouldn't mind just staying here. Would you mind? I'm sure Gramps wouldn't."

Bev wanted to believe Kevin wouldn't mind, but he had put her in charge of Katie until he returned. "Are you sure? I don't want to do anything to violate his trust of me."

"I think if he knew we'd been up talking for four hours straight, he wouldn't mind at all."

Bev weighed Katie's angelic response with the gnawing feeling Katie was playing her. "I hope I'm doing right by your grandfather."

"Can you tell Gramps that my staying here was your idea?"

"Ha! No chance." Bev headed for her bedroom to get ready for work. "I'll just give the diner a call and let them know I had extenuating circumstances preventing me from coming in on time today. I'm glad your grandpa owns the place. If I'm late many more times, I could get fired."

"May I cook some breakfast for us? I'm pretty good in the kitchen. Just tell me where everything is, and I'll get busy."

"Absolutely. That sounds like a good idea." Bev directed her to the kitchen and opened the refrigerator door. "Other than the cereal and pancake mix, which you'll find in the cupboard above the stove, all my food is right here. I have turkey bacon, eggs, turkey sausage, fruit, just about anything you could think of. Surprise me. I'll get dressed and be back out."

Katie began unloading the food as Bev headed for the bedroom. "I wonder why Gramps hasn't called us yet."

Bev stopped at the bedroom door. "Maybe he's not up yet, or maybe he thought he'd wake us up if he called last night. Could be, he's turned off his phone. I hope he took the time to get some rest somewhere."

Katie peeled the plastic apart at the corner of the package of bacon and pulled the top layer off. "If I know him, he's been worrying all night."

Bev knew Katie and Kevin were much alike. Even though she was still a teenager, teenagers had plenty of worries. Maybe Katie shouldn't be left alone for even a short time today. "On second thought, I have plenty of vacation days coming. Why don't you and I contact that decorator lady today? Wouldn't that be fun?"

"I'd love to. But can we talk to her on no sleep?"

"Ha, we'll see. Maybe our adrenaline will keep us going for a while; however, I won't do it on an empty stomach. Show me what you can do out here while I make myself presentable. I don't want this decorator lady to see me at my worst again."

Katie's welfare seemed wrapped up in Jenny's. Bev hoped and prayed Kevin had been able to make progress with the authorities concerning Jenny. For one as meek, gentle, and compassionate as Kevin, Bev worried about the problems with the women in his life: one floating here in Lake Serenade and the other treading water in Tallahassee. If Kevin couldn't resolve Jenny's situation, he'd have another crisis to face when he got back.

Chapter 12

"I love this ride across the Escambia Bay, especially when the water sparkles so with the sunshine." Bev hit the power button to lower her window.

Katie crouched in the back seat, where she attempted to change into fresh clothes. "To be honest, I get a little squeamish on bridges, but I'll try to look at it when I finish. Thanks for stopping to get my clothes."

"You're welcome. The bridge is safe; it's a brand new bridge rebuilt after Hurricane Ivan blew through here in '04."

Katie climbed back into the front seat and stared out the window. "I would have been ten, Bev. I don't remember too much about that."

As soon as they had crossed to the other side, Bev powered her window back up and pushed the AC button. "We're almost to our turnoff."

Dressed in a pink halter top and blue-jean cutoffs,

Katie positioned the lever on her vent until it faced her and directed the cool air into her face. "I'm glad Hattie was able to finish up in Wisconsin and get back here so quickly. I would have hated to wait at the airport."

"Acting as her personal taxi service will give us more time to get to know her." Bev pointed to a green Exit sign. "Isn't this our turnoff?"

Katie smirked as a hint of sarcasm slipped from her lips. "I'm not from here; you are."

"Humor me, Katie; I don't get to spend all that much time talking to people." Bev chuckled as she took the tight curve on the exit ramp then noticed the hotel straight ahead on the right. She headed south for a short distance then turned right into the hotel parking lot.

"All joking aside, I'm telling you, you have more in common with my grandpa than you think."

"Such as?"

"Such as your preoccupation with nature. Is that what happens to people in their fifties?"

"I know you're joking with me, but people in their fifties just happen to have a good handle on what life is actually about, such as appreciating the things God has created."

Katie moaned. "Bev, I suppose you're going to tell me I don't have a handle on life."

Bev pulled into the first available space and turned off the motor. "I think you do pretty well for your age. Anyway, time to change the subject. We're here, and I think Hattie's standing under the hotel canopy."

"She looks pretty bright for someone who's taken a red-eye flight."

"I think she flew early to save time. Hand me my purse, please. It's on the floor behind your seat. I want to make sure I have the notes your grandpa wrote out."

Katie twisted behind her and grabbed the rope-wrapped handles of Bev's large red canvas bag. "This is heavy. What do you carry in it?"

Bev reached for the handles. "Just a few snacks." She rummaged in the purse, pulled out her billfold, two packets of cheese and crackers, a banana, and one apple, placing the snacks on the console. Katie peeled the banana and took a bite as Bev sorted through the bill compartment for the folded piece of paper. "Is this the note?" She pulled out the paper on which Kevin had scribbled his ideas and skimmed over them. "Wow, I hope he doesn't go through with all these changes."

"Let me see." Katie swiped the paper from Bev's hand. She read part of his plan then looked at the woman standing under the hotel awning beside two paisley-print, expandable suitcases with inline skate wheels and telescopic handles. The shoulder strap of a bright pink bag looped around her shoulder. "You're sure that's her?"

Hattie looked similar but different than she did the first time Bev had met her. Her hair, still blond, now had a swatch of hair sprayed or dyed pink—a pink that matched her purse. Bev stifled her chuckle and took the note back. "That's her. I only saw her once when she came into the restaurant with your grandpa. Isn't she lovely? Let's hope she has something better to offer than what your grandpa has planned for the diner." Bev opened her door. "Let's go have a look-see."

Katie opened her door, got out, and followed Bev's lead. "You talk, okay? You know what Gramps wants."

Bev meandered between two rows of parked cars and became more tentative as she got closer to Hattie. "Me? I think we'll just play it by ear and see what Hattie has to offer."

Katie hurried to keep up. "He did seem like he wanted change, but all we talked about is how I didn't want him to make any changes. I love the diner just the way it is. It could be a blessing in disguise that Gramps's not here. That could be good."

Bev loved the way Katie's thought process worked. Could they be any more alike? Bev continued to the curb and gave Hattie a nod and a smile as she approached the hotel canopy. What would walking in her shoes be like? Hattie was creative, unencumbered, had a successful decorating business, and a man waiting for her beck and call. "Good morning."

"Oh, you're that sweet little waitress from the diner." Hattie stepped off the curb to meet Bev. "I remember you now. I'm Hattie Lincoln." Hattie stretched her hand out, and Bev and Hattie shared a warm handshake while Katie stood beside Hattie and waited.

"I look a little different without my uniform on."

Hattie waved a hand in the air. "Oh, that's no biggie. You're just doing what your former boss wanted you to. Maybe your new boss will be more stylish."

"I'm so glad we were able to catch you before you purchased a bus ticket," said Bev.

Hattie fluffed her hair. It fell to her shoulders with youthful, horizontal crimps running parallel to each other at regular intervals. "Bus ticket? Ma'am, I'd rent a cab before I'd ride a bus."

"Oh, just as well. Anyway, I'm glad we had a chance to greet each other informally at the diner. I hope we'll be able to make some strides with this decorating project Kevin has initiated. Nevertheless, the ride back to Lake Serenade will be much more pleasant than renting a cab or riding on a hot bus with smelly bathrooms."

Hattie folded up the edges of the sleeves on her pink,

pointelle-stitch sweater and pushed each of them up past her elbows. Then she put her arm around Katie. "And who might this young one be? Don't tell me. You're Millie Sample's granddaughter, aren't you?"

Katie nodded and then took hold of both suitcases and turned them around. "I am. May I take these for you?"

"What a sweet child. She's so polite isn't she, Bev?"

Bev couldn't have been prouder of Katie than if she were her own granddaughter. She only hoped Hattie didn't go to extremes and try to pinch Katie's cheeks. "She certainly is. Follow me, Hattie. I'm parked in the last row."

"I can tell you this. I would have known Katie anywhere. She resembles her grandma so much."

"That's quite interesting." Katie chuckled as she continued to the back of the car.

"Why is it interesting, Katie?" asked Bev.

Katie wheeled the suitcases around to the trunk. "It's just interesting; that's all."

Bev shrugged, pressed the key fob to open all the doors, and then tossed the fob to Katie. Bev opened the driver's door and watched as Hattie followed Katie to the trunk to show her exactly how to position her luggage.

Katie did as she was directed then closed the trunk and tossed the keys to Bev as Hattie walked to her door. "I guess I'm ready to head to that adorable town of yours again."

Bev raised her brows at Katie then got in and started the car. She opened her window a crack to allow Hattie's perfume to escape then turned on the air. "You don't mind air-conditioning, do you, Hattie?"

"I use air when I'm in Florida," said Hattie as she adjusted the lever to blow the breeze away from her face. "I don't use it all the time out on Hilton Head where I live. We have such a nice breeze. I hate to ruin the natural air with artificial cool air. This is a nice car you have, but I'd think that boyfriend of yours would buy you a brand-new one, Bev. He used to promise a car to me all the time."

Katie muffled a laugh in the back seat. Bev frowned at her in the rearview mirror as she pulled out of the parking lot. "This is a rental car. Katie and I own it only for the day, and that's all. Mine's not as comfortable as this one."

Katie leaned forward in her seat. "My grandpa offered you a car?"

Hattie laughed. "Not in the way you think. Your grandma, Millie, had two cars. One of them she drove for every day. It barely putted along. The other one was a used VW convertible. Kevin offered me the clunker if I'd redecorate a business lobby of his up in New York. I demanded cash instead." Hattie rummaged around in her bag and fished out a nail file, which looked like a bejeweled piece of sandpaper with numerous pink glass shapes decorating the handle. She began scraping the file across the ends of her nails. "Never take gifts from a man you don't intend to spend your time with."

As Bev accelerated onto the interstate, she caught Katie's eyes in the rearview mirror and issued an eyebrow warning to her not to say anything else. Meanwhile, she mulled over the thoughts pounding in her head. Should she invite Hattie to stay with her while she was in Lake Serenade? However, could Bev tolerate a perfume-induced migraine until Hattie finished with the diner? She could try. "Hattie, if you don't have a place to stay I'd be glad to loan you my spare bedroom if you want. I live alone."

"You what? You mean you and Kevin aren't… ? I mean, I assumed you and he were an item since you showed up here with Katie. You know, maybe you and Kevin lived together and Katie lived there, too."

Bev bit her bottom lip and raised her brows as she engaged the cruise control and digested Hattie's last comment. Maybe Katie would jump in here and answer so she wouldn't have to.

She raised her eyes to the mirror to find Katie in the center of the back seat with her head resting back into the groove between the two headrests. Her mouth hung open in a death pose, and Bev realized she couldn't rely on Katie for any assistance. "Hattie, can I be honest here, woman to woman? I don't know how to explain my relationship with Kevin. He certainly is a nice man, and I'm glad to know him, but my future is in God's hands. I just try to live my life and wait for Him to show me what to do next."

"Oh no." Hattie slumped down in the seat and shook her head. "Why do I always end up having conversations with people who know God?" She held up her hand and counted on her fingers. "First, my friend Emily, then Ted, the guy I met down on Anna Maria Island, and my cousin in Georgia, and now you. Can't I just once find some friends who want to talk about men or decorating or the beach?"

"I'm just saying Kevin and I have only known each other a few weeks. I work at the diner he wants you to decorate, and we're becoming close friends. He couldn't be here today, so Katie and I answered his plea for us to meet with you. He and I do not stay together in the same house."

Hattie relaxed into her seat. "Okay, honey, I was just askin'."

Bev couldn't help but notice the grin on Hattie's face. Maybe if Bev sat quietly, nothing else would be said regarding Kevin.

"Where is that delightful gem, anyway? Don't you think he's cute? Is he working at the diner? You know, I've never known a man to get as involved with his businesses like he does."

Bev stifled her need to let this woman know she and Kevin did have something going on, and they did spend time together, and they were headed in a good direction. She wanted to share with Hattie how he kissed her cheek and held her in his arms, but she didn't want to be arrogant or catty. She'd just have to hope for the right moment and let the facts speak for themselves. After all, Hattie did have her sights set on another man—didn't she?

"May I help you?"

Disheveled from his hasty journey the night before, gray stubble peppering his upper lip and cheeks, Kevin cleared his throat and tried to state his case. "I'm here regarding Jenny Johnson. I believe she's being held."

The woman at the desk was dressed in normal street clothes: a long-sleeved, green polo and black slacks. A high-heeled, toeless shoe occasionally bobbed out from the bottom of the false front of the desk. "You look tired." She motioned to the thick wood chair sitting adjacent to her desk. "Why don't you sit down? Can I get you a cup of coffee?"

Feeling underdressed in his sweats, he lowered himself into the chair and looked at her name tag. "I'd love a cup of coffee, Miss Osgood, but I'm parked out front in a two-hour-limit parking zone."

She shuffled her feet, rested her hands on the desk in front of her, and stood as she leaned sideways to see out the front door. "You'll be alright out there. Linda Martin has street duty today. She doesn't usually get started with the chalk marking until around ten, and she starts at the far end of town first." She pointed to the clock on the wall behind him. "It's only nine-thirty. Excuse me for a moment?"

Kevin nodded his head as she disappeared through the door on the far side of the room next to where two uniformed officers sorted through a pile of paperwork.

Jenny was his only child. He longed to see her come out of this fog she seemed to be in, come to their home in Lake Serenade, and settle down to the task of raising Katie. Even though Katie would be heading off to college in a year, it was never too late to get down to the business of family. Jenny needed Katie and him both. How would she find her way otherwise?

Within minutes, Miss Osgood came back through the door with a steaming cup of coffee in one hand and a couple of creamers and sugars in the other. "Here you go. If the heat doesn't jar you, the coffee is strong enough to wake the dead." She set the condiments on her desk and moved some paperwork to make room for the cup. "Now, tell me again, who is the person you're after here?"

Kevin balked at her lack of memory. Maybe she needed coffee worse than he did. Nevertheless, he couldn't refuse the coffee. He peeled back the lids from the creamers and emptied both into the cup. "Jenny Johnson. I received a call from her last night asking me to come up here and help her get out of jail. I came up after I got her call, but the office was closed, so I waited in my van all night. If you could simply tell me what she's done."

Miss Osgood took a pad of scrap paper from her top right drawer. "And your name, sir?"

"Sample. Kevin Sample."

"May I have your driver's license, Mr. Sample? Your relationship to Jenny Johnson?"

Kevin took his billfold from the sweatshirt pocket, removed his license, and handed it to her. "Father. I'm her father."

After studying the license, she copied his information, handed it back, and drew a double line under his name. "Wait a minute. I'll go grab her paperwork and be right back."

Kevin began to steam almost as much as the coffee. *A quick trip. Why couldn't this have been a quick trip? I have to deal with a bunch of paperwork gurus who don't care that I've spent the night in my car.* He took a slug of his coffee then a deep breath. She was right about the coffee being strong. The brew tasted like bitter pencil lead mixed with acid. With any luck, it'd clear the gunk from his teeth left over from the pizza he'd had before a night of sleeping sideways across the front seat of the van.

Shortly, Miss Osgood returned then settled down into her chair. After she shuffled through her paperwork, she smiled and looked into his eyes. "Alright, Mr. Sample, the bond on your daughter is fifty thousand. You pay five thousand, and she's out of here. I'll give you a sheet of instructions on what to do once she's in your custody."

Kevin shoved his chair out so quickly it toppled to the floor. "Why so much for a few traffic tickets?"

Miss Osgood stood and hurried around her desk as the two officers on the far side of the room hurried to Kevin's side in a split second. "Mr. Sample," she said. "This is not about any traffic tickets. Yes, the traffic tickets and parking tickets are outstanding, but those allowed us to take Jennifer into immediate custody. Surely your daughter told you the real reason she's sitting down the hall."

Chapter 13

"Lahmeyer residence."

"Katie, it's Bev. Just wanted to check on you. Everything okay? Are you feeling better?"

Katie giggled. "Yes, and I heard from Gramps. Isn't that the real reason you called? He got to the city building in Mundy around midnight. He didn't want to wake us, so he waited till today to call."

"If only he knew how long we stayed up. Where did he stay?"

"He slept in his car overnight."

"Oh dear. I bet he's not too alert right now. How's your mom?"

Katie hesitated on the other end. "He didn't say. How's Hattie doing?"

Bev's heart dropped. Katie deserved to know the details of her mother's arrest. She deserved to have her mother back here with her. "After I took you home, I dropped Hattie off at the diner and ran some errands. I just got back." Bev pushed the front door open at the diner and walked in. "I hope she's making progress. She wanted to interview everyone who came in today, to see what they did and didn't like about the diner. She's in a conversation with the Bradleys right now. They own the new bed-and-breakfast up the creek a mile."

"What do you want to bet she talks a room out of them? She's quite the charmer."

Katie was right. Hattie was quite a charmer. Bev wondered how much of a charmer their new decorator had been with Kevin. "Katie, I only stopped by to talk to Nora. I'll be back in a jiffy. Why don't you try to catch some sleep while I'm gone?" She remembered well the first day she saw Kevin and Hattie. They were quite an attractive couple. First impressions had a way of sticking with a person.

"Okay. I'll be here. Try to find out where Hattie is staying tonight. If she stays here, can I stay, too?"

"She told me on the way here she had a reservation at the motel at the south edge of town. She may change her mind. I'll let you know. See you soon."

Bev stuffed her cell back into her purse as she made her way across the diner to Nora. "Did I hear you say you were heading home and leaving me here to entertain the stranger from South Carolina?"

"Sorry, Nora. I have to make a request of you. Kevin headed out of town for a day or so, and Katie is staying with me. I need to figure out how I can take a couple days off. You think someone could come in and work for me?"

Nora raised her brows then winked. "Hmm, I wondered if things weren't going to start brewing between you and the new boss. I'll see what I can do."

"No brewing here. He's entrusted Katie with me. If you can't get me a couple days, I'll bring her in here. She'll do fine helping out for a few hours here and there."

Nora laughed and gave Bev a hug. "It's Thursday, and weekdays have been slow. You weren't on the schedule, anyway, for today. You need off until Monday?"

"That would help tremendously."

"You don't look too good. Is something wrong?"

What could she say? Plenty was wrong. She tried to dismiss the thought that another woman in town might be after Kevin. She didn't want Nora to recognize her concern, nor could she reveal to her anything going on in Kevin's family. "Ah, nothing like that. I woke up during the night and never did get back to sleep. I think the lack of sleep's catching up with me."

She hated not confiding in Nora. The two of them had shared so many of life's ups and downs over the years. However, her loyalty in this matter belonged to Kevin and Katie. For now she had to bear this one alone.

Nora waved her away. "You go on, now. Katie at your place or are you going to her house?"

Bev put her arm around Nora's shoulder as they walked toward the door. "She's with me. I need to get back home and keep her company."

"You mean, keep the boys away?"

Bev smiled. "Something like that. See you Monday?"

"Okay. Get some rest."

"Since Hattie is very engrossed with the Bradleys, I'm not going to interrupt her now. Tell her, if she needs me, to call."

Nora moved Bev toward the door. "Will do. Now get out of here."

Bev headed out to her car. She let out a sigh and

combed her fingers through her hair. Something didn't feel right about Jenny's arrest. Kevin took the situation hard, but Bev had begun to think something much graver than traffic tickets were tying Jenny up in Mundy.

Kevin and Katie both needed Bev right now. Grandfather and granddaughter were masters at hiding their pain. As she shook her head in commiseration, the thought overwhelmed her that she needed Kevin and Katie. Maybe, somewhere along the way, she and Jenny would need one another, too.

Kevin followed Miss Osgood down a long hallway sporting high ceilings with peeling paint. Swallowed up by the unforgiving narrow walkway, he could have stretched his arms out in a line with his shoulders and touched the wall on either side with a flat palm. The Mundy building was reminiscent of the old courthouse in Lake Serenade with its ornate fruit designs and artists' renderings on the ceilings.

Tamed by the presence of the two police officers sandwiching him between their solemn gait, one between him and Miss Osgood and the other behind him, Kevin dreaded what he would find once they got to the room where he was meeting with Jenny.

Driven by his business acumen, he hurriedly created a bulleted list in his mind of what he would address with Jenny. Number one: What on earth was she thinking? Number two: Didn't she know she'd be caught? Number three: Didn't I raise her better than this? Number four: She should have been home with Katie instead of gallivanting around the state capital doing research. He just as rapidly crumpled the mind list and dropped it in an imaginary wastebasket.

Miss Osgood stopped at the end of the hall, fifth door on the right, and tackled the ring of keys attached to her belt. Eventually, she found the key she wanted and slipped it into the lock. "This way, Mr. Sample. Your daughter is in here."

The two officers accompanied Kevin into the room while Miss Osgood headed back down the hallway. His vocal chords stuck together as he searched for a way to greet Jenny. He expected tears, repentance, and hugs from her, but the lack of those disappointed him. Whatever he'd say, he knew the words had to be gentle and accommodating. "Jenny, are you okay?"

Jenny sat behind a four-by-four wooden table embedded with grooves of graffiti, scratched-in and penciled names, and four-letter words he didn't want to read. Her hair was disheveled; the light blue cashmere sweater with tiny pearls sewn across the yoke from one shoulder to the other was soiled; and the dark mascara on her eyes was smudged. While she sat motionless, with her hands folded on the table, her expression told him she refused to be joyful. "Have a seat, Dad. I know you must be tired. I'm fine, but can you get me out of here?"

She sat in the room like a teenage girl who'd just been caught sneaking into a five-dollar movie instead of a grown thirty-eight-year-old woman with a teenager. Kevin measured his words as he pulled out the chair and sat down. He'd do anything for her, but why didn't she seem to realize the magnitude of this earth-shattering act of irresponsibility?

Her life had seemed to fall apart after Carl's death. Was Carl the reason, or had other things come into play, such as the recent inquiries she had made to Kevin regarding their family background? He'd learned to shield most of her questions but knew he'd eventually have to give an accounting of the facts. "Of course I can. It'll take me a few hours to get my finances organized, but I'll post bond as soon as I leave here."

She drew her hands from the table and muttered peevishly under her breath. "We have a lot to talk about. Are you up to hearing what I have to say?" A raspy chuckle followed. "Imagine that. I'm starting to sound like you. How often have I heard you say the same thing to me? Anyway, my life has changed from this point on. I think you need to know what has happened to me in the last forty-eight hours."

Kevin sat across from her, his eyes haunted with inner pain, as she explained what she'd done, and hoped she'd look at him. He expected some kind of reconciliation before he left. Jenny and he had always had a tight bond and an understanding between them. She usually felt free to talk to him, just as Katie did now. What had happened? Even though Jenny had made her own decisions, he felt guilty because of his own past. After she'd let him know she'd finished, he scooted away from the table and stood. "I'll get right to it, Jenny. I love you."

One of the officers escorted Kevin out of the room, down the hall, and to Miss Osgood's desk. She motioned for him to sit and explained to him what his responsibility would be, from this point—where he needed to go to get bail and how long he had to get it. Most of her oratory escaped him because he was engrossed in his own plan. As soon as the woman was finished with her dialogue, he'd be out the door and on the phone to Bev.

He wished Bev was here now. Her soothing presence, her wisdom as she spoke all the things he once knew about God but had forgotten, and her kindhearted expressions of friendship had already worked their charm on him. He wanted to be near her and feel her bolstering support and assuring him everything would work out, and hoped she'd tell him she'd be a breath away for him if he needed her. He wanted to feel her closeness and hold her in his arms. He did need her. He couldn't live without her.

Chapter 14

"Gramps tried to call you on your cell." Katie poured Bev a glass of iced tea and handed it to her. "He sounded a little distraught when he called."

Bev took a sip of tea and set the glass on the counter. "I think my cell is in here somewhere." She set her purse on the counter and felt around inside, stopping to take out two church bulletins and two packs of crackers. "I know it's in here somewhere."

Katie shoved an empty glass into the chamber on the front of the fridge and filled it half full of ice. Then she emptied half the ice into her glass and the other half in Bev's tea. "He said he called at least three times. Must have been important."

After an unsuccessful search, Bev finally dumped everything on the counter top. "I found my phone." She picked up the red-sequined, two-sided case that protected her smart phone and pressed the Home button. "Well, three recent calls from your grandfather. I'd better get back to him right away, and then you and I can talk about things."

"Things?"

Bev gave her a sheepish grin and she pressed the button to call Kevin. "Things."

"He called me once and you three times. Hmm. Wonder what that means?"

"You are a relentless cupid. Your grandpa wants to talk. The fact he's called three times tells me the urgency, but he's not answering now. I hope all is well." Bev pushed the End button and laid the phone on the counter. "Did he have anything to say about your mother this morning?"

Katie took her tea and headed for the dining room. She pulled out a chair and sat down at the table. "It's what he didn't say. He wouldn't tell me anything. You'd think he'd realize by now I'm not a child. I can take whatever he has to tell me."

Bev took a drink of her tea and joined Katie. If only Kevin could see Katie for whom she was life would be easier for both of them. "You're smart and know more than most girls your age. I have to agree with you. I don't know why there has to be a generation gap."

"You had no children, right?"

Bev picked up her glass and swallowed her tea so fast she almost choked. Katie's words sounded like a death sentence—as if all women were *supposed* to have children. She had always wanted some of her own and dreamed of the day when she'd have at least two daughters.

However, Huff had found out early in life he could never father any children. Bev knew the situation when they married and figured God knew what He was doing when Huff came into her life. She looked up at Katie. "I had no children with Huff; however, I think I'll adopt you. You have been a loving delight for me ever since I first met you. Isn't it crazy someone could affect me that way?"

Katie repositioned herself and tucked her leg up under her body. The sparkle in her eye told Bev she was up to something ornery. "Bev, I feel the same way. I'm so comfortable here. I hope Gramps gets wise and asks you to marry him."

"Whoa there, not so fast. I think he has a say in this, too. Besides, don't you see the picture? Our friendly decorator has seen fit to stay in town a couple extra days. I think she's quite interested in one Kevin Sample." Bev drank the rest of her tea and wondered if she had been too transparent with Katie.

Katie sipped at her tea, her eyes dancing with laughter. "Don't worry about Hattie. According to my grandfather, she's just a friendly person who likes men. I had a long talk with him. He insists she's just a nice flirt."

"I understood she had a man friend around the Anna Maria area. Wasn't his name Ted, or something like that?"

Katie's mouth fell wide open as her face glinted with pleasure. "You're jealous, Bev Lahmeyer. You're afraid Miss Hattie has come to town to sink her teeth into Gramps, and you can't handle the competition."

Bev gave an angelic smile as she pushed away from the table and took her tea to the kitchen. "That's ridiculous. I just wondered about her, that's all."

Katie followed her out to the kitchen and topped off her glass of tea. "I may be young, but I'm quite aware of what's going on inside people's minds and hearts. You're anxious he might be interested in someone else, and you haven't been with anyone for so long you don't know how to respond. For my sake don't back down now."

Bev raised one eyebrow in a questioning slant. Her cover had been blown. She had admitted to herself her attraction to Kevin. "Back down? I'm not the one who's been making all the moves."

Katie's face beamed as she rested her hands on Bev's shoulders. "Hey, Mrs. Lahmeyer. You didn't seem to be disappointed when he placed his hand against the glass that one night or was about to kiss you last night."

As Bev searched for the right words, the phone rang. "I'll get it."

Katie reached for the phone first and checked the caller ID. "It's Gramps." She handed the phone to Bev.

"Hello?"

"Bev? This is Kevin. Do you have a moment?"

"Of course. What's happened at the jail?" Bev motioned for Katie to come closer and pressed the Speaker button.

"You're not going to believe this," he said. "My common, ordinary, never-would-hurt-a-flea daughter has been arrested for breaking and entering. I nearly passed out when I got into her holding room and she told me. I'm broken over this."

Katie grabbed her stomach and backed away.

"What? Where are you?"

"I'm in my van just leaving the city building in Mundy, and I have to make bail."

Bev's intuition told her there could be a connection with Jenny and the robbery at Bev's attorney's office. Her heart pumped spastically. She glanced at Katie out of the corner of her eye. "Wait, tell me again."

"This is the last thing I thought I'd be doing in my

life—getting my only child out of jail. Do you think I'm doing the right thing? Should I leave her to simmer for a while before I bail her out? Help me, Bev. I trust your judgment."

A sudden knot twisted Bev's stomach as she pressed the Speaker button off. The news regarding her files being stolen from her lawyer's office was so fresh in her mind she couldn't wrap her thinking around the possibility that Kevin's daughter could have been the one to break into the law office. No, Jenny's dilemma was only a coincidence even though both happenings were in the state capital at the same time. Coincidence? No, she couldn't have committed a robbery. Someone made a mistake. Surely this was all erroneous information. "Kevin, I don't believe any daughter of yours could have done such a thing. From all you've told me about her, I think they must have the wrong person."

Tears pooled in Katie's eyes. "What, Bev? Why is she there, then?"

Bev paced from the kitchen to the laundry and back and mouthed the words, *I'll tell you in a minute.*

"I wouldn't have believed she could do such a thing either," said Kevin. "In fact, I decided not to believe the charges. Then I visited with Jenny in one of the holding rooms. She is a thief. She told me so. She just wants out now, and she says she'll give me details later."

"Do you even know where she was when she got caught?"

Katie headed out to the lanai.

Kevin moaned and exhaled a breath of air. "Nothing. I'll know more later. I'm going to get the money together for her bail and get her out of here and back to Lake Serenade. Do you think I'm doing the right thing by her? Am I being too lenient? Maybe I should insist she spend some time in jail and think about her actions."

Bev walked out onto the lanai, digging her nails into her palm. She wished a way existed to have gone with him, but she couldn't have accomplished any more than he did. Only Jenny could decide when and where she would talk. "No, Kevin. No, you're doing the right thing. Let me know any way I can help out. Katie is here. She's fine. Just call us whenever you want."

His voice quavered. "Can you keep this from Katie?"

Bev glanced over to Katie who had taken a seat in one of the wicker chairs. "I don't see how I can. She already knows, and I believe she can handle the truth. Anyway, she heard most of the first part of your conversation. I didn't feel she should be left out. You have a grown woman on your hands over here, and she will handle the news better if you don't keep her in the dark." She winked at Katie. "She loves you, and she loves her mother."

At first, Kevin paused; then his voice seemed distant. "Okay. I'll let you do as you feel best. Just pray all goes smoothly."

Bev fought to keep the hitch out of her own voice. The trail they were blazing was awkward, yet she raised her chin in determination. "You mean what you said about praying?"

"I mean what I said. I may have kept God at bay in the past, but I know God is the only one who can get us all through the next few days. I give you my word."

"S'pose that little alligator will come swimming when he sees my toes dipping into the water?" asked Katie.

Bev laughed as she slipped out of her tennis shoes

and sat down on the dock next to Katie. "I don't think so. He's not aggressive; he's just curious. Now, momma gator, she's the real problem. If she thinks junior is in trouble, we're in trouble."

"I don't see them anywhere."

"I haven't seen her yet."

"How do you know she exists?"

"Others in the park have seen her. Up till now, we all thought the little guy was a pet someone set free. Then, they saw momma. They still think the gators were pets. What gator would have babies this time of year? Unless the conservation officer got to them, they're in the rushes up there somewhere, but I wouldn't worry. They won't bother us out here on the wharf."

"I had a friend who told me a story about an alligator who swam in a pond of water in someone's mobile home park in Alabama. They fed him marshmallows. Whenever any of the kids came to visit, their grandparents took them to the pond to feed him."

"Ooh, now, that's dangerous. You can't keep a wild animal penned in a pond just for fun." Bev rolled her pant legs up to her knees and settled her feet into the water. "I haven't done this for a long time."

"So, tell me more about the phone call." Katie fluttered her feet back and forth in the water.

"This is all I know, Katie. Your mother is in trouble, and your grandfather is worried. Here's this lovely, innocent young woman he's brought up from infancy who is now going out and doing things she normally wouldn't have considered doing."

Katie lifted her feet out of the water, pushed herself back on the dock, and tucked her feet under her body. "She's my mother. What aren't you telling me?"

Katie was still in that innocent stage of life—believing the best of everyone, not blaming anyone for life's drama she had experienced so far. Bev hated to drop the curtain on her purity of soul. Bev pulled her feet out of the water and sat cross-legged. "Your mother was found taking some things that didn't belong to her. You heard that part. Your grandpa says it's true. Your mom told him as much. He's torn now. He doesn't want to rescue her without her learning a lesson, yet he doesn't want to leave her to face this alone."

Katie's bottom lip trembled. "That can't be that she stole something. Maybe she just borrowed them. She was doing research up in Tallahassee, you know."

"Jenny just asked him to get her out of jail; then she will tell him the rest of the story. None of us knows any more than that." Bev bit her lips together while she waited for Katie to respond.

Bev still held out hope Jenny wasn't the person who broke into her attorney's office. Jack would have called her to let her know if they had someone in custody. She couldn't allow herself to marry the two circumstances. *It just can't be the same person.*

Katie clutched her arms around her stomach. "I don't know if I want to know any more than that. When will they get back? Did he say?"

Bev stood up and brushed off the back of her pants. "No, but I'm surmising they won't be back till late tonight. Want to stay the night again?"

Katie sucked in a deep breath and rose to her feet. "I'd love to, but I don't think I'll get much sleep. You suppose Gramps will call me when he gets into town?"

"You know him better than I do. It's just my guess he'll want to get your mother settled first, but I could be completely wrong on that issue. Let's find something to eat for dinner and wait for his call."

Katie looped her arm through Bev's. "Thank you for trusting me. You gave me information my grandpa thought I couldn't handle. That's why I say you and I could be family. Even though Gramps and Mom aren't here, I feel like you and I are related, and I feel kinda needy right now. Being with family is the only thing I would want tonight."

Bev squeezed Katie's arm. "We are family. We'll eat and then see what else happens. If everything goes well with the bail and getting her things from her motel, they may just show up early."

"I'll help you with the meal. We may have another night of talking ahead."

"We can eat, talk, sleep, or do whatever you want." The wounded look in Katie's eyes broke Bev's heart. She hoped just to get the teen through the night. Once her mother got home, Katie could talk to her. "Katie, don't worry. God has everything under control."

Chapter 15

Last night's thunderstorm left little reason to take the shortcut to Kevin's house. The road would be nothing more than a cow path covered with mud. Going by way of the highway took an extra ten minutes, perhaps fifteen, since Friday traffic always increased in both directions this time of year. "Katie, did you call the diner for me to tell them I'd be late?"

"This traffic is so slow. I wish we could have gone the other way. Yes, I called work for you. Do they know what's going on with my mother?"

Bev slowed with the traffic. "I wouldn't tell the people I work with something this personal. They don't know what's going on. The less they know the better. And thanks for calling in for me."

"Thanks for letting me stay one more night."

"Your grandpa and mother probably can't wait to see you."

Katie's face brightened with a broad smile, the first Bev had seen from her in days. "I'm glad my grandpa called me last night when they got home."

Bev followed traffic as it veered left to avoid a large pool of water in the street then picked up speed after they passed the flooded area. "Did you talk to your mom at all?"

"No, but I heard her in the background talking on her phone."

"She may have been talking to an attorney."

"I can't wait to get home and find out why she would do such a thing."

"Don't get your hopes up. You might not find out much more than you already know."

"I can't wait for her to meet you."

"Katie, listen to me a second. Things are in an up- heaval right now. I don't think this is a good time for introductions. I don't think your mother even knows I exist other than being a friend who helped you out in a rough situation. I'm going to drop you at the driveway."

Katie gave a pained expression and leaned against the door. "But I want you to be in on this."

"Honey, my involvement isn't important. You have your time with your family so you can heal from this ordeal. I'll get together with you when you've resolved the situation, okay?"

Katie stared at her, a stress line forming on her brow and her shoulders bowing in surrender. "I guess that makes sense."

Bev looked in her right side-view mirror and moved into the right lane of traffic. Within a few minutes, she pulled into Kevin's driveway on the right. She put the car in Park but let the motor idle. "Be merciful, Katie, and lean on the Lord. He'll get you through this. They both need you right now. You may be the only stable factor between the three of you."

"I will. Thanks." Katie hugged Bev then opened the door and got out. She scurried up the walk but slowed and paced herself up the steps, onto the porch, and in the door.

Bev's stomach clenched out of sympathy for Katie. She put the car in gear and backed out into the street. As she drove off, she took another look at the house and caught a glimpse of Kevin opening the door for Katie. Then, she saw him wave. Bev hit the Power button on her window, thrust her arm out, and raised her index finger in the air to let him know she saw and understood. She had to go back.

By the time Bev got turned around and parked at Kevin's, he had walked down the sidewalk to the driveway. She was glad for the unexpected opportunity to speak briefly with him and pulled into the drive, parking next to where he stood. "Hi, Kevin. How are things going this morning?"

He slowly shook his head. "Those were a long two days, but being back together and trying to communicate is going better than I expected. Jenny's beginning to open up, but I just wanted to talk to you a minute." He massaged his lower back. "Boy, if you ever get a chance, don't spend the night in your car."

Bev stifled a laugh as she stared proudly into his eyes. "I can imagine sleeping was pretty painful."

"It was. I don't plan on sleeping there again anytime soon."

"Let's hope you don't have to."

He leaned his hands on her car door. "I just wanted to tell you, my heart skipped a beat when I saw you pull out of the drive. I realized while I was gone just how much I like being with you."

She chuckled. "Kevin, you weren't gone for that long."

"No, no I wasn't, but I sure could have used a friend to lean on while I was away from home."

She patted his hand. "I feel the same way. Taking care of a teenager is much more difficult than being with a class full of them in Sunday school for one hour."

"Did she give you trouble?"

Bev shook her head. "Oh no, nothing like that. She's just an amazing young woman and has a lot to say. The difficulty came in trying to say the right things to her."

He raised an index finger and nodded. "Ha, you were living in my world for a couple days."

Bev clasped her hands together and slanted her head to make eye contact. "Just a side note here: Don't feel pressured to say anything about me to Jenny."

"She'll know who you are once Katie gets a hold of her. I wouldn't doubt but what she's filling her in right now."

Bev swallowed dryly. "I better go."

He nodded. "I understand. I'm glad to have seen you no matter how briefly."

She knew exactly what he meant. Just this short time together had been nice, but they'd have more days of separation ahead. If a stronger relationship with Kevin lay ahead for her, she'd need to find some sense of normalcy herself. That involved getting back into her routine of day-to-day life. "I'll be praying for you three over the next few days. I believe a lot of good things will happen in a short time."

"We'll have many chances to be together, Bev. Once things get back to normal, I'd like to visit your church.

You know, get back to the things I once held dear. Thank you for understanding."

His voice sounded constricted, and she knew this was probably one of the most difficult times he'd faced in his life. She gave a quick shrug of her shoulders and bit her bottom lip as she looked up into his eyes. "Your family needs this time together." She hesitated. He'd gone through Millie's death, Carl's death, and now the death of the closeness he'd once had with Jenny. Yet Bev felt the need to keep a door open for him. "You just call me if you need me, Kevin."

He reached through the window and stroked his fingers down the side of her face. "I'm glad you came back by. I'll stay in touch."

After he walked back up to the house, she backed out of the driveway and headed home. She had some serious thinking to do. While everything within her wanted to believe Jenny was innocent, the more she went over the story in her mind, the more she realized Kevin's daughter may have committed the crime. In fact, Jenny may have been the one to rob Bev's attorney's office. There was only one way to find out. She had to go further than home. She had to head up to Mundy.

"Nora, are you sure Mattie doesn't mind working in my place?" Bev couldn't get back to any routine until she'd found out who the thief was.

Nora put her arm around Bev's shoulder and walked her to the door leading out of the restaurant. "Both of my kids are home on break for the summer, Bev. Mattie has two more weeks before she heads back to school. She'll be glad to fill in for you while you're gone. You just be careful, and try to get some rest. You need your sleep! Now get on out of here and head for your cabin."

"Thanks, Nora. You're a good friend. I'll let you know when I get back." Bev headed out the door and got in her car to drive home. While Kevin and his family met together, she'd visit her attorney's office then spend a few days at her cabin.

With nervous anticipation, she headed back home to get ready for the trip. If Jack didn't want to be forthcoming on the phone about how much information the thief had acquired from Bev's files, she'd show up at his office in person and demand an accounting. She had to get confirmation that Jenny did or didn't break into the legal offices.

After packing an overnight bag, she grabbed her laptop then headed out the door. She made sure the house and shed were locked and then drove down the street to Robert and Helen's house to let them know she'd be gone.

As she slowed in front of their home, Robert gave a wave. "Going shopping?"

Bev rolled down her window. "I'm going to be gone for a short time. I just wanted you to keep an eye on the place while I'm gone."

"I hope you're not driving that thing. Do you want to take mine?"

She waved him off. "I've reserved a rental downtown. I'll head to get the car after I leave here. Thanks anyway."

"Sure enough, I'll take care of your place. You be careful, and don't worry about anything."

"You call me on my cell if you need anything while I'm gone." Bev gave a nod to Robert then raised her brows to Helen. This was the only thing she didn't love about this place where she lived. Just when one got to know people, they left—whether physically or mentally—for good.

An overwhelming aroma of artificial balsam hit Bev as she walked into the Hibbert and Kindler Law Offices in Mundy. The odor-covering smell seemed reminiscent of her school days and the sickening pine-scented soap with which they had cleaned the floors.

The office lighting was set on low, and no one sat at the receptionist's desk, but Bev heard conversation and laughter coming from down the hall to the left. Given it was the noon hour, she assumed they'd all gathered for lunch in one of the conference rooms. She remembered where the room with the microwave and apartment-sized refrigerator was due to the hours she had spent here when she and Huff had come to plan their estate.

She peered around the corner and down the long hallway to the room at the end where the occasional secretary or business associate appeared behind the open door, some with coffee cups in their hands and some with food. Knowing the staff wouldn't see her out here unless she made herself known, she headed down toward the conference room.

Alicia greeted her as Bev stopped short of going through the door. "Mrs. Lahmeyer. What can we do for you today?"

Bev smiled her greeting and noticed Alicia's quick nod to someone else in the room. Before long, Jack, with paper and pencil in hand, peeked around the doorway. "Bev. Come in. We're just taking a lunch break. Have you eaten?" As if she were a long-lost friend, Jack merged her in with the rest of the staff by taking her hand and introducing her to the others.

Feeling self-conscious that she had obviously interrupted this chatty legal crowd who had suddenly become silent, she excused herself and pointed over her shoulder that she'd head back down the hallway to the reception area. It was amazing to her how one could develop an inferiority complex when set in the presence of so many educated people.

Jack closed the door to the conference room behind him and followed her out to the reception area of the office. He set his tablet on the reception desk and stuck the pencil behind his ear. "You don't look too happy, Bev." He waved his hand toward another room. "Why don't we go to my office? I gather from your intense demeanor you've come to talk whether I want to or not. Nevertheless, I have an hour before my next appointment, and we'll have more privacy."

She nodded her head as her heart pounded. Finding out the truth wasn't always a good thing, but finding out the daughter of a friend was a suspect in the robbery was worse. She shuddered to think she would soon know, *if* Jack was forthcoming with the information. "Good enough for me. Lead the way."

Jack directed her to the door straight ahead and opposite the receptionist's desk. He stuck the key in the lock and opened the door to reveal a few pieces of heavy oak furniture and unadorned walls. Before he walked in, he switched on the light then motioned for her to sit in an overstuffed, brown leather chair. "Make yourself comfortable, Bev. We have things to talk about."

Bev took a deep breath and focused on the myriad of law books adorning the three levels of wood shelving in his office giving the otherwise austere room a touch of professionalism. She settled into the chair and folded her hands in her lap while her eyes settled on the full box of books on the floor that had three upside-down frames piled on top. "I know a good decorator, if you need one."

He made a pained expression before his eyes darted from one corner of the room to the other in appraisal. "This is the disgrace of being a bachelor attorney. Everyone wants to tell me how to decorate, but no one wants to pitch in and help."

"Okay, I'll get off the subject and get to the reason I'm here, Jack. What do you know about my records?"

"I figured that's why you came." He walked behind his desk, removed the pencil from his ear, and tossed it on the desk. He put his hands on his hips and made eye contact with her. "This one thing I do know: The thief got away with your entire file. But I imagine the good news will make you happy." Jack took a seat in his black leather revolving chair and rolled it to the desk.

He leaned his arms on the desk while clasping his hands together and focused on his hands as he opened and closed his fingers. "Emily, the girl who worked here before Alicia, had set up an elaborate code when she filed all my cases. While the thief got all the paperwork describing your court proceedings, your wishes, and your family's wishes"—he paused to look her in the eye—"she didn't get any names."

"What? Why were mine the only ones taken? Doesn't that seem suspicious to you?"

"They didn't just take yours. The thief took off with approximately seventeen folders at least." He cleared his throat twice. "All but yours were outside the window on the ground. The police assumed the robber dropped some of them from the window, returned to the file cabinet to get more, and repeated the process. The job was clumsy. The security guard happened to walk past the door at the precise time the thief slammed the file drawer closed. The departure out the window was hasty, to say the least."

Bev shook her head to get the smog out of her mind. "Why those particular seventeen folders, Jack, if the names weren't on them?"

"They were all filed under the letter 'R.' Your maiden name, Ryan, is the name we've used in the electronic files."

"And the robber has mine? Including my court papers?"

Jack pushed away from the desk, left his chair, and headed out to the reception office. Bev heard him open and close a file drawer before he brought a folder back into his office. After he closed the door, he handed the folder to Bev. "Here. We recreated this file from your info stored on the computer, for the benefit of those who detest looking up computer files. We've recreated all seventeen folders and have filed them back in the same spot. You can see there's no name… ."

"The name doesn't matter at this point."

"Your name was on nothing in your file."

"But, my personal life is represented in that file. If the right person were looking, he or she would know who I was by reading the court papers."

"You could have called me. I would have told you over the phone."

Bev tapped her heels nervously on the floor. "*You* should have called *me* with this information. I needed to come in person to satisfy my own questions since you hadn't called. Is the suspect in custody?"

"This is going to be the hard part, Bev. They caught her."

A sudden spurt of adrenaline coursed through Bev's

veins as she forced a swallow down a dry throat. "Her?" She watched with numbed horror as Jack picked a newspaper up from the floor.

"Listen to this: 'Former New York native, thirty-eight-year-old Jenny Sample Johnson, was arrested late last night for the robbery attempt at Hibbert and Kindler Law Offices in Mundy, near Tallahassee. Ms. Johnson's bond was set at—' "

Bev felt faint. "No, Jack!"

Jack tossed the paper on his desk. "You remember that name, don't you?"

She stared him down as she felt some of what Kevin must have experienced when he found out Jenny had been arrested. A sudden unknown enemy compressed all the air from her chest and wouldn't release its grasp. Her words came forced and slow. "You didn't press any charges, did you?"

"Bev…"

Jack tried to take her hand, but she pulled away. "Please tell me you didn't press charges."

Jack crossed his arms and sat on the edge of his desk. "Of course, I pressed charges. This is a serious offense. She committed a robbery. You can't break the law simply to satisfy your own inquisitiveness."

"But, you know why…you know why she did it." Suddenly everything became perfectly clear to Bev. Kevin Sample unexpectedly showing up from New York with daughter and granddaughter in tow. A golden opportunity opened up for Jenny to do research close to her father's hometown—the father who adopted her. Bev knew all the answers now, and she didn't know if she could ever face Kevin again.

She'd had suspicions when Jenny was arrested but had dismissed them. She'd wondered what would ever possess a young woman with all the advantages that Jenny Johnson had to commit a robbery. Jack didn't have to tell Bev anything else. Bev knew the answer. Jenny Johnson was the child she'd given away at birth, and Kevin Sample was the man who had pulled her daughter from her arms, illegally.

Chapter 16

One night at the hotel in Mundy was long enough to stay away from home. Bev would put her visit to the cabin on hold until she could get home and pack more things to take with her. Soon, she'd travel away from Lake Serenade for a long time.

Realistically, she'd known, deep inside, this moment could come. She didn't understand that making her secret public would be so emotional and life destroying. Why did all the other things, like falling in love with Kevin, have to come before?

As soon as she arrived in town and exchanged her rental for her own car, she headed home. Once she pulled under her carport, she noticed a note taped to her lanai door. Robert ambled up from his home at the same time Bev got out of the car. "Don't want you to think I didn't watch out for the place. The woman who put the note on the door seemed so nice and all. I didn't think it would hurt to allow her to do it."

"Woman?" With Robert following behind, Bev walked around her car to the door and lifted the scented pink envelope. She recognized the fragrance as Hattie's. She gave the note a slow, appraising once-over and adjusted her sunglasses, glad they hid the dark circles under her eyes. "When did she come, Robert?"

"Last night around the supper hour. She was mighty pretty, and I've never met anyone so kind. Said she was leaving town to head for Anna Maria Island down south. Asked me to give this to you, but I brought some tape up and told her to put it on your door."

The first smile of the week spread across Bev's face then quickly disappeared. She opened the envelope and took out the note paper. Hattie said she'd only found one thing to change in the restaurant—the cash register. She loved the decor because of the nostalgia, but she hated the computerized cash register, which didn't fit the scheme. "Well, well, well. What a surprise."

"Everything okay?"

"Let's just say, something is okay, and I was wrong about so many other things. How can we misjudge character so badly sometimes? Thanks, Robert. I have a lot to do. Give Helen a hug for me."

Robert gave his quick wave and headed back home. Bev unloaded her suitcase from the car then walked into the lanai, locked herself in, and headed for the kitchen. After she'd put a pot of coffee on to brew, she rolled her suitcase into the bedroom and stashed it in a corner. Bev headed for the closet and turned on the light.

As she looked for more clothes to take with her, the memory box on the top shelf on the left drew her attention. Huff was with her when she'd opened it last. Bev had wanted to share her past with him. But opening the box now wasn't about sharing her past anymore. She had to come to terms with her past. She had to revisit the memories before she left town.

She moved three plastic containers full of pictures and stacked them on the floor on top of one another. Then, she lifted out the cardboard box of photos and memorabilia and set it on the floor by itself. After she turned out the light, she carried the box out into the living room and set it on the wicker coffee table in front of the loveseat. She was about to turn a light on the darkness of her past.

Before Bev opened the box, she got her dust rag from the broom closet and wiped across the top of the lid. She dropped the rag to the floor, plunked down into the loveseat, and eased off her tennis shoes, sliding them under the couch. She stared at the box as if the memories inside were enemies to be avoided, but she had to dust off the remembrances *inside* the box as well.

After three shrill beeps from the coffeemaker had alerted Bev the brewing had finished, she shuffled into the kitchen, oddly aware that she had passed over some kind of hump in her life. It was a strange feeling. Soon her hidden past would be out in the open, and her daughter had been the instrument to make it happen.

She turned the pot off and poured the coffee into a carafe then opened the refrigerator to find milk. After she'd poured the milk into a small ceramic creamer, she brewed another pot of coffee. She picked up the carafe, slipped her little finger through the handle of her Florida Gators mug to carry it, and took the creamer with her into the living room. After she'd arranged them all on the side table and poured herself a cup of coffee, she settled in.

The cellophane tape on the box had yellowed and curled at the edges but held the ends of the deep twelve-by-fifteen-inch box closed securely. She took a deep breath and began to remove the first piece of tape then the next and the next.

The musty odor of memories long forgotten greeted her nostrils as she peeled back the flaps of the box. She stared at the white tissue paper tucked neatly around the voluminous treasures inside for a moment then poured another cup of coffee. After a sip or two, she set her coffee cup down and began the task of revisiting the memories.

After she pulled out the tissue, a bit of nostalgia hit her when she focused on the two yearbooks in front of her. By the time she had gone to high school, the officials had turned high school into a three-year program. Ninth grade in the seventies was still spent in junior high. The yearbooks from junior high, the fancy paper-bound books with black-and-white photos, were packed away in another box. This box held the genuine treasures.

These yearbooks were special. They were hardbound and represented a certain rite of passage into the upper grades. She pressed her palm against the cover of the red yearbook then ran her fingers across each raised letter of the Lake Serenade High School *Legend* from her sophomore year. She'd worked an extra week after school at the Ice Cream Palisades downtown just to pay for the *Legend*.

After she had set it on the floor, she lifted out the green yearbook from her junior year, also embellished with raised letters of the school and yearbook names, but these letters were edged in silver. This one had even more memories attached to it, since she had just made

the cheer squad and even had the basketball players'
signatures in it. But the senior book was missing.

By the time the yearbook had come out in the spring
of her senior year, she'd already withdrawn from school,
and her shamed parents wouldn't allow a child of theirs
who hadn't completed the senior year to purchase it
either. She set the green book down on top of the red.

When she lifted off another layer, she found a few
trinkets and souvenirs she had collected from field trips,
vacations, and special moments, arrayed in a perfect
row across the length of the box. One was a miniature
likeness of the Statue of Liberty in New York City,
where she had traveled with her parents while she was
still in junior high school. Another souvenir was a tiny,
black, ceramic doll with a red dress dotted with white
circles from New Orleans. Still another was a piece of
petrified wood from the forest in Arizona she had visited with her parents when she was four years old. These
were meaningless to her now.

Underneath all the souvenirs lay a small five-by-
six-inch box around which she had wrapped white tissue. The tissue seemed new and hadn't yellowed at all.
She slid the tissue off the box and removed the lid to
reveal a worn black-and-white photograph marred by
hundreds of pin holes. The successful dart-throwing
campaign had done little to harm his likeness, but at
least her actions had soothed her heartache. One of the
photo's corners was bent over and had nearly broken
off from years in the box. Stephen Fisher had ruined
her life—and she had let him.

Sure, it may have been childish for a seventeen-year-
old girl to carry on so by cellophane-taping his photo
on the back porch woodwork and tossing darts at it, but
she had good reason. He had hurt her in a way no one

had ever hurt her before. Stephen had led her to believe she was the most beautiful young woman on the earth. He had rescued her from all her years of abuse with her father. He had been a safe haven. Even though she felt in her heart Stephen wasn't the man for her, she made her alliance with this rescuer—for all the wrong reasons.

He'd convinced her to run away and get married in their senior year. Being married felt right. They'd driven off in his red-and- white '65 Camaro, which he'd spent the day waxing. He'd bought her a dozen red roses—the most fragrant she'd ever smelled—to hold when they stood in front of the judge. She'd picked out a silver friendship ring she'd admired from the five-and-dime store, and he'd put it on her finger after they'd said, "I do." When they got back home and announced their news to their parents, Bev's mother and father had the marriage annulled.

She straightened the corner on the photo and pressed down some of the holes. His timing had been terrible when he told her his family was moving. Of course, at that age, you couldn't refuse to move when your parents did. She and Stephen had exchanged addresses so they could write to one another. At first, she thought he'd follow through on his promise to write her, but he'd sent her one postcard depicting the flower children of the Haight-Ashbury neighborhood with the inscription indicating he was about to join them. She knew then he'd never return to Lake Serenade. That was the second time she'd thrown darts at his picture.

She had kept his picture this long for only one reason. Somewhere in the recesses of her mind she thought it best because she had a soft spot for the person he was to leave behind. She'd kept the photo, not for him but for the sake of the child that grew inside her.

He'd sent her this one photo. He'd grown his hair longer. She imagined he probably made a good hippie with his love for freedom. She stared at the colorized photo depicting his auburn hair pulled back into a ponytail and the cowlick in his long bangs on the left side of his forehead. Now she understood why Katie had looked so familiar to her. Katie resembled him to a *T*. Little did he know this photo would confirm Katie's link to him.

Bev laid the photo aside on the arm of the chair and took the empty carafe back into the kitchen, where she filled it back up with more coffee. She took a cleansing breath and looked out the window. She'd miss living in Lake Serenade. With a full pot of coffee, she returned to her loveseat.

Most of the boxes remaining inside held various photos of her growing-up years. She extracted one more layer of tissue paper. The only photo from her senior year in school found residence in the silver box tied with silver cord, a gift from one of the nurses at the hospital. She held the box in her hand and stared. This would be the hardest box to open.

A flare-up of emotion waited to erupt in her heart, but she had no tears for the picture in this box. She untied the elastic cord, laid the cord on the arm of the chair, and opened the box. If she could computer-optimize the photo inside to what the baby girl would look like today, hands down, it would look like Jenny Johnson.

Bev winced at how easily one person could find another, even when they'd covered their tracks so perfectly. Somehow, Jenny had found information that led her to Bev's attorney's office. *How* was no longer the issue. The fact remained, Jenny *wanted* to find her.

Bev lifted the picture of little Jane Elizabeth, the

name Bev had given her, from the box, and studied it. Even though the photo was in black-and-white, Bev saw it in color. Only Jane's pudgy cheeks peeked out from the tightly wrapped white blanket edged with two pink stripes. A pink knit cap covered her hair, dark from the day she was born.

The day had been so painful. No one had explained to her what having a baby felt like, yet Bev lay in the hospital with great expectations ready to go through anything until the labor pains hit. Now, in numbness, Bev shook her head as she laid Jenny's photo on top of Stephen's. The emotional pain had been even greater.

Neatly folded under the photo was a newspaper clipping from New York, which featured a story about Jane when she was a little girl. The picture of the three-year-old was in the box also. Jane had been photographed as the winner of a three-legged race at a Boy Scout picnic in Essex County, New York. Somehow, the story had made its way back to Lake Serenade, probably because the parents had been natives of this area. While the paper didn't name the father and mother, Jenny Sample was listed as the child. They'd changed her precious name.

Bev put the clipping back into the box, set the box on the arm of the chair, and then bent over double and wept. *Why now, God? I did Jane a favor and stayed out of her life. I wasn't supposed to ever see her again. I wasn't supposed to ever know who her parents were. Now, just when I have seen a new chapter evolve in my life, You make this new man of mine the adoptive father of my daughter? I don't understand. I cannot face him with this. What must he think of me, knowing I was the girl who gave her baby away to complete strangers? I will never know happiness with him now and will never know Katie's love.*

She'd given up her daughter, and she had to come to terms with her decision once and for all. What could she do now to alleviate Jenny's pain? She left the room and her memories, taking her coffee mug, the creamer, and the carafe to the kitchen, where she set them into one side of the double stainless steel sink. Without another thought, she picked up her phone, made a call to Jack Kindler's office, and hoped he was in on a Saturday. Whatever the cost was, she had to get Jenny cleared of the charges.

Chapter 17

Dressed in khaki walking shorts, a green T-shirt, and flip-flops, Jenny walked out the door onto her front porch. She pulled the towel from her damp hair and made a beeline for Kevin. "The grapefruit grove smells wonderfully fresh." She stopped abruptly and pointed to the open Bible on his lap. "That's nice to see."

He gave her a smile and a nod of his head.

Katie left the rocker she had been sitting in and gave Jenny a hug. "He doesn't know I know, but he usually sneaks mine and looks at it."

Kevin turned his attention to Katie and frowned. "Have you been spying on me?"

"No, you just don't put my Bible back the way it was before you took it."

"I don't deserve you or Gramps, little one," said Jenny.

"Come on, Mom. Let's sit down in the swing like

we used to do when I was little. Gramps moved it all the way down here from New York. Sort of nostalgic, right?" Katie walked Jenny across the porch, but Jenny stopped in front of her father.

"You both seem so forgiving of the mess I've created. I think I'm ready to talk, if you're ready to listen."

Kevin marked his place with a piece of yellowed paper he'd written a Bible verse on years earlier. "*If we confess our sins, he is faithful and just and will forgive us our sins and purify us from all unrighteousness.*" Kevin knew God had given him a wake-up call when Jenny got in trouble. He had sidestepped his relationship with Jesus for a long time. Now Kevin needed Him and His direction for their lives.

As the man of the family, it was time he acted like it. Next week at this time, he'd take Katie and Jenny to church. He looked up at her. "I should have listened years ago, honey. I think I speak for both Katie and I now. We want to hear what you've been going through."

Jenny and Katie walked arm-in-arm to the wooden porch swing that was suspended from a four-legged iron frame much like that of a children's swing set. They sat down, and Katie began to gently push it back and forth as they looked out over the lawn.

"Can you move your chair closer, Dad?" asked Jenny.

"I would be happy to." Kevin tucked his Bible under his arm and turned the chair around to face both the girls. "How's that?"

After he sat down, Jenny reached over and patted him on the arm. "Perfect." She leaned back closer to Katie, who had now taken her mother's hand. "Dad, since the day you and Mom shared with me about how I had been adopted, I hadn't wanted to find the woman who gave me up. Doing that had never crossed my mind.

I was so deliriously happy with you as my parents that I could care less about anyone else."

Jenny, the adult, faded into the background as Jenny, the pigtailed twelve-year-old with her hands always busy doing something, came into view. Her hair color hadn't faded much, she still had her youthful skin, and she would always dig at the very depths of his heart. He'd take care not to judge, not to point the finger, and definitely not to jump to conclusions. No more bulleted lists about what she should and shouldn't do. He'd been waiting for this moment a long time. "Is finding your birth mother what all your research was about?"

Jenny nodded. "It hit me after Carl died how quickly life can fade away or disappear. I suddenly had this ache in my heart that I couldn't reconcile. I was elated to find out you wanted to bring me and Katie with you when you moved down here."

"Me, too, Gramps," said Katie.

"Dad, I needed to find her my way, so I launched out on my own once we got here. The more I found out about her, the more I wanted to know. I know from my research of the local church records and chamber of commerce that this town is where you both went to church and worked. I didn't want to pawn Katie off on you, but I couldn't seem to stop myself. Does such a thing exist as becoming addicted to research?"

Kevin shrugged his shoulders. He'd been addicted to work. Wasn't that one and the same?

"Eventually, I became obsessed. To make a long story short, my research ultimately led me to the attorney's office. I'd found many tidbits of information and eventually linked them all together. I found that most of the information I wanted was right here in Florida. Can you imagine that?"

Kevin swallowed hard. Nothing was out of reach for a ravenous researcher. He shook his head.

"Dad, please don't think me flippant about this. I've ruined my life, and I'll have a record forever. I know that, but I don't know how I can ever apologize to you and Katie and convince you I mean it."

"You should have just come to me. I would have helped you."

"I was afraid to ask you. You'd kept it a secret from me for a long time, so I started asking questions around various places throughout Lake Serenade. You know, if you ask enough questions in a small town, the gossip will eventually give you some answers. Little tidbits I'd picked up here and there led me to the library in Tallahassee and ultimately to my birth mother's attorney in Mundy. I knew I had to get those records from him. I was willing to do anything to read them, and look where it got me."

Kevin's heart stood still. Jenny had set her own course in this matter. Nothing could be done to wipe her name from the arrest records. He wanted to reassure her he wouldn't abandon her, even with the evident trial ahead. Still, he had to address her heart, to see if she even knew what was inside. "Was it worth it?"

"I hated every aspect about the arrest. It was so degrading, and I think I'll be okay no matter what kind of jail time I'm looking at. I can't backpedal, Dad."

Beads of perspiration formed on Kevin's forehead. Was he up to knowing where this woman—Jenny's birth mother—was or who she was? He couldn't even remember her name. "It sounds like you've found your natural mother."

"Yes. She still lives right here in Lake Serenade."

An imaginary arrow pierced Kevin's stomach, to

think the woman whose child he raised had been here right under his nose. He'd assumed she'd long since moved away. Did she know who he was? "Lake Serenade?"

At the same time, Katie jumped to her feet. "I have another grandmother, and she lives in this town? Who is it?"

"She works at the diner you bought, Dad. Her maiden name was Beverly Ryan. Her married name is Beverly Lahmeyer. Do you know her?"

Kevin lay sleepless in bed soaked with sweat, his eyes burning. He couldn't remember the last time he'd cried so hard.

He and Millie had both put that day from their minds—the young high school girl being restrained by her mother and father as Kevin and Millie took their precious Jenny from her arms. They'd agreed to allow the mother to hold her newborn baby one more time before they took her and left town. That picture had stayed in Kevin's mind throughout Jenny's childhood. Once she progressed into her teens, the scene eventually faded, and Kevin moved on.

His precious Bev had kept this terrible memory in her heart for nearly forty years. Did she know her child was Jenny? Was she aware of the unthinkable events of the last few days? How he wanted to be with her and hold her and tell her how much he appreciated her allowing Jenny to have a better life. On the other hand, he assumed Bev hadn't given her baby up willingly—something he needed to share with Jenny.

A knock on his door preceded a whisper. "Gramps, are you awake?"

Kevin sat up in bed. He didn't want to talk to Katie.

His shame over the way he'd handled the adoption process had humiliated him and had come back to haunt him. How could he face her now that his soul was convicted and his eyes were inflamed from weeping? He raised his voice enough for her to hear. "Not now, Katie. We'll talk in the morning."

Another knock. "It is morning, Gramps."

Kevin rubbed the flakes of sleep from his eyes and glanced at his clock. It was only three in the morning. He got out of bed, pulled on his robe, and made his way to the armchair that sat next to an open window and sat down. "Come in."

Katie pushed open the door slowly as she entered the darkness. "Where's the light?"

"Do we need it?"

"Are you going to make me sit in the dark?"

"Turn on the floor lamp to your left."

Katie switched on the light and took a seat in the chair next to the lamp. She stared at him for a moment, as if she wanted to cry with him. Then her eyes widened. "Wow. Can you believe what happened tonight? My natural grandmother is Bev. Maybe that's why we hit it off so well."

Kevin cleared his throat. "Katie, I want to thank you for not telling your mother about Bev and me…us. I think we need to let her take the lead in contemplating the information she already has and reveal our bit of news to her later."

"Gramps, I don't think you're being very wise. I think we should tell her everything. This changes who we are and how we identify with Bev. I mean, she's actually my grandmother, and I'm dying to tell her."

He cleared his throat again. "Not yet. Giving your mother up was very difficult for Bev. So many thoughts have plummeted through my mind about that day and the whole arrangement. I'm certain this will bring up a lot of pain in her heart when she finds out."

Katie pulled her feet underneath her and stared across the room at Kevin. "Can you tell me what happened?"

"No, I don't want to tell you what happened. I'm not very proud of the way the whole thing was handled."

"Gramps, my life has changed in the blink of an eye, and you won't let me know how it happened? Perhaps Bev will tell me."

Kevin shifted in his chair at her haughty remark and tugged the belt on his robe tighter. "Katie, don't go pestering Bev." Kevin wasn't sure he wanted Katie to hear the story from Bev's point of view yet. "I'll tell you, but you're not going to be happy with me."

"I love you, Gramps. What could change my love for you?"

"Tell me the answer to that after I finish." He cleared his throat. "You see, your grandmother Millie had met Bev's mother at a church function. When Bev's mother found out your grandmother—your grandmother Millie—wanted to have children but couldn't, she had a thought that perhaps we could adopt Bev's baby after it was born. Bev's mother didn't want a baby around, and our accepting Bev's child was easier than going through an agency."

"Is that why you and Grandma left town after you got my mom? Was it too painful to stay here?"

He blew out a spurt of air. "It worked out that way. We didn't know the girl, and I'd already been transferred to the New York area. We held off moving for two weeks while we waited for your mother to be born because she arrived two weeks past the due date."

"What about my grandfather? Who is he?"

"We were never told, honey. All I know is Bev and he had been married for a few days. Her mother told me she and Bev's father had the marriage annulled since both Bev and her husband had been underage."

"How sad. Was the adoption legal, then?"

Katie had hit a sore spot. At the time the "adoption" took place, he hadn't worried whether or not it was legal. Millie was so happy to hold a baby in her arms; he didn't want anything to change that. He couldn't answer Katie. "It's nearly daybreak, Katie. Why don't you let this troubled man sleep for a while? We'll talk about all this after we've had some breakfast later."

Katie stood and turned out the light. "I think you just answered me, Gramps. I can't believe you and Grandma would have done something illegal to get a child. Especially to someone as nice as Bev. You have just broken my heart. I'm not sure how I feel about this whole situation, and I don't know how you'll ever be able to sleep again."

As the door slammed behind Katie, the wrongfulness of it all brought so many more problems to bear. But above all, how did he fare with God on this matter? What had *He* thought about the swift actions in removing a weeping young woman's child from her arms and leaving town? Kevin had carried the guilt over taking the child all these years. Jenny wasn't legally his, and now, Katie didn't want him.

Chapter 18

Light spilled in through Bev's bay window on Monday, signaling the short amount of time she had to get out of town. She'd already taken an extra day to write notes and instructions to the park's manager regarding her hope to come back before long to get the mobile home ready to sell. She'd also take the time to contact Nora before she left town.

Before long, Kevin would be nothing but a memory. He wouldn't want to be with her once he found out she'd been married twice and had given birth out of wedlock, but on the other hand, he and his wife had taken Jane Elizabeth from her arms. Bev couldn't face the certain turmoil that would accompany any further contact with him, and she couldn't take a chance on Jenny finding her. She had to erase Kevin from her mind.

She'd had her doubts at the time her baby became Kevin's but could do nothing to stop the turn of events that followed. Her mothering instinct had told her not to give Jane up, but Bev's mother told her she'd already signed legal papers. Perhaps her mother was the only one who could've stopped any adoption from taking place.

Tears came to her eyes. Would Jenny ever know Bev didn't want to part with her? Would Kevin tell her the truth about that day? Whether only a lead or actually Bev's name, Bev realized that Jenny had been trying to find her. Why else would she risk her future and break into an attorney's office? *I know she's my daughter. I want to see her so badly but can't.*

She jumped at the knock on her lanai door. *Lord, please don't let it be Kevin.* Bev wiped under her eyes then headed for the lanai. As she peeked around the corner, she saw Nora. Bev quickly headed for the door to open it. "Nora? What are you doing here?"

Nora threw her arms around her. "I hope I'm not interrupting your vacation. I just had to talk to you. Is it a bad time?"

If Nora knew she had planned on leaving for more than a vacation, Nora would set up a road block bigger than the county sheriff would do. She released the embrace and motioned to the chairs in the lanai. "Let's sit here. How about a cup of coffee?"

Nora sat down in Huff's chair and shook her head. "No, thanks. I just finished my fast-food coffee and muffin."

Bev positioned the other chair to face Nora then sat down. "What brings you here so early, girl? Don't you have to be at work?"

Nora gave her an inquisitive smile. "I switched with someone else. I wanted to whizz by here and see if you were okay, and now I see. You're desolate."

Bev pasted on a smile. "I'm okay. I'm just tired and need a break. What could be wrong?"

"You've been taking a lot of time off work."

"Can't a person take her vacation?"

"Look me in the eye, Bev. Tell me you really needed a break from work and that's why you took time off. Tell me you all of a sudden decided you didn't like your job anymore and had to get away."

"What?" Bev knew where Nora was headed with her line of questioning. They'd just talked a few months earlier about how their jobs helped to keep them young and feeling alive. They'd jested that they'd allow their vacation time to accrue so they'd have two months to get away to some exotic destination down the road.

Nora took on a serious look. "I want to know what's wrong. It's not like you to call at the last minute and say you won't be in. I've been by here a lot, lately and have stopped to talk to you. You're never here. I even cruised by Mr. Sample's house to see if your car was there. What's going on?"

Bev stared past Nora and focused on the azaleas next door. "I have nothing to say."

"You have nothing to say? Then tell me why we've been getting phone calls at the diner from someone named Jenny Johnson. Is she part of this mystery?"

Bev's voice cracked. "She's calling at work for me?"

"Okay, so you do know something. Besides that, the color drained from your face when I told you she'd been calling."

"Come in the house. I want to show you something."

Nora followed her into the living room and sat opposite Bev in the old recliner. "What's this?"

Bev gathered the photos together and handed them to Nora.

Nora raised her brows. "Who's this boy all covered with holes? Looks like you were really mad about something."

Bev stared at the photo. "That's Stephen. He and I were married for a few days when we were in high school. My mom and dad put an end to it, but not soon enough. Look at the next photo."

Nora laid Stephen's photo aside and looked at the baby's photo. "You're not going to tell me this is your baby, are you?"

A tear rolled down Bev's cheek. "That's Jane Elizabeth—a.k.a. Jenny Johnson."

Nora moved to the loveseat beside Bev and put her arms around her. "Oh Bev, are you telling me this is your baby, and now she's here trying to find you?"

Bev sniffed back her tears and moved away from Nora to avoid her provoking any more tears. She sat in the recliner. "Nora, here's the bad part. Jenny Johnson is Kevin Sample's daughter. I'm in love with the man who took my baby from my arms thirty-eight years ago. How could this happen? How can we ever continue any relationship together?"

Nora dropped back against the cushion. "How could he have taken her from you?"

Bev shook her head. "It was my parents' doing. They arranged it and executed it before I could even say a word. It was the darkest moment of my life…until now."

Nora pointed to the two suitcases standing near the dining table. "You're not just leaving on vacation, then, are you?"

Bev shook her head. "I don't have time to pack everything now. I'll do it another time. But I can't face Kevin right now knowing he's the man who took my child away."

"Bev, we're back to that trusting God thing again. Don't you think if God has arranged all of this so far, then He has a plan for the next chapter?"

Bev wanted to agree with Nora. Everything in her heart told her to hold on, talk to Jenny, and listen to Kevin's side of the story. "I believe He does, Nora, but I don't know what Kevin's thinking at this point. I don't know what he and his wife had to say about my situation the day they took Jane. What if I agree to wait around, and I get knocked in the teeth by his rejection? What then?" Bev got up and walked out to the lanai.

Nora followed and took her hand. "Here, sit down and take a deep breath."

Nora sat next to her. "We're going to talk this situation over, and after we're finished, you're going to ask yourself a few questions. What was it in the beginning that drew you to Kevin? Did you believe in him then? Did you think you could do life with him when everything was rosy? If so, what is keeping you from doing life with him now that everything's in turmoil? I ask you, Bev. Is he worthy of your love, and are you worthy of his?"

"Time for a family meeting." Kevin yelled from the bottom of the stairs, hoping to rouse his daughter and granddaughter from their sleep. The nicer way would have been to go to their rooms and give a gentle wake-up call, but he had no time.

Before long, Katie's galloping strides sounded as she took two steps at a time landing both feet on the oak floor at the bottom. She tugged her sweatshirt on over her long-sleeved T-shirt and zipped it halfway up. "Sounded like a camp counselor rousing the kids. Can I at least get a cup of coffee first?"

Kevin pointed to the kitchen. "It's freshly made." He turned his attention back to the stairs, hoping Jenny hadn't decided to skip town and disappear from their reach. After about five minutes, he made another call. "Sleeping Beauty, we're waiting for you."

Katie carried a mug of coffee to the living room and snuggled in the brown suede chair in the corner. "I think Mom must have gotten more sleep last night than she's had for weeks."

Kevin stuck his head in the stairway then looked back at Katie. "I hope she's still here."

Katie took a sip of coffee and pointed to her mother's Gucci purse on the dining room table. "Don't worry, Gramps. She wouldn't have left without her designer purse. Besides, I don't think she's a flight risk."

Kevin joined Katie in the living room. "Thanks for admonishing me last night. It's always a shame when someone so young has to prod someone my age into being a man. I'm going to tell your mother—and you— everything this morning."

Jenny entered from the stairway. "What is it you're going to tell me, Dad? Do I have time for coffee first?"

He nodded. Mother and daughter were so much alike. He wondered what things they had in common with Bev. When Bev got wind of *who* he was, she might not want to know about any similarities. She might close the door on him forever. He'd deserve it.

Jenny carried the pot of coffee, a ceramic mug, and a carton of milk into the room with her. "Where can I put this?"

Katie pointed to the coffee table. "How about on the table in front of Gramps?"

Kevin took the milk from under her arm and set it

down in front of him. "That will work fine, honey. Just make yourself comfortable."

"How comfortable? Are you going to make me wish I'd kept this all to myself about finding my birth mother?"

"Mom, just relax. You're going to want to hear this."

Jenny shook her head and pulled up a chair opposite Katie.

Kevin wrung his hands together as he focused on Jenny's face then on Katie's. He turned back to Jenny. "Honey, I want you to know all the circumstances surrounding your adoption."

"Dad, it's kind of late for that."

"But we weren't always forthright about everything. We were sworn to secrecy, signed a document saying so, and were never to bring up the subject of your natural mother again."

"What? Says who?"

"Mom, will you be quiet, please, and let Gramps finish?" Katie let her eyes drift back to her grandpa. "Go ahead."

Kevin smiled inside. Katie could be his worst enemy or his best friend, depending on how the mood hit her. He continued to wring his hands together and kept his face down. "I'll just try to tell it in story form. A long time ago, two young teenagers fell in love. They wanted to be together so much that they ran away to another state where they could legally get married. Happier than cats in a tub full of catnip, they returned home to let everyone know what they had done. The young woman's parents were outraged and even threatened the boy with arrest."

Katie scooted to the edge of her chair. "Oh no, that's so sad."

"The girl's parents got the marriage annulled. I don't know what happened after the annulment, except the boy's family left town and headed out West. My wife— your mother, Jenny—met the girl's mother at a church function. According to her, she hadn't separated the two teenagers soon enough. The girl was pregnant, and the boy didn't know."

Katie and Jenny sat spellbound, right up until the very end. Kevin hesitated to finish, but he knew he had no other choice. God had brought him to the place where he had to tell the complete truth. Otherwise, their family would be in more upset than he wanted to face. "The girl's name was Bev." He gave a nod to Jenny. "Now I know that Bev is the same Bev you've found."

Jenny scooted up to the edge of the couch and set her mug on the table. She leaned her elbows on her knees and covered her mouth with her hands, and then she eyed him skeptically. "She didn't want to give me up, did she?"

Kevin exhaled a deep breath and massaged the area above his cheekbones to avoid her gaze. "She was forced to do so. I imagine a young girl of sixteen or seventeen in that predicament has little to do but give in. Her parents literally ripped you out of your mother's arms and handed you over to us." He looked at Katie. "Now you know."

Katie wasted no time in getting to her grandpa and threw her arms around him. Jenny just stared for a few seconds before she joined them on the couch. After crying together for a few minutes, Kevin took Katie's and Jenny's hands. "I'm sorry, girls. I'm so sorry."

Jenny looked him in the eye. "I love you, Dad, and I forgive you, but I want to see her. I've called the diner, and she hasn't been to work. I don't know where else to look. Do you have any ideas?"

Katie nudged Kevin. "Gramps has one more thing to tell you about Bev. Don't you, Gramps?"

Jenny's phone rang. "Get that, Katie, won't you?" She looked at Kevin. "What else do you need to tell me, Dad?"

He steepled his hands and tapped his fingers together. "I had no idea who Bev was. We've been seeing each other."

"What? How much more tangled can this get, Dad? Do you think she'll want to see you when she finds out who you are?"

In seconds, Katie reappeared. "Mom, it's for you. It sounds official."

Chapter 19

"Oh Nora, is it worth it? I appreciate your advice, but I think I just want to fade into the background and let the past rest."

Nora stood to go. "The young woman has been looking for you. Doesn't that give you a chill up and down your spine? You have responsibilities now, whether you want them or not, whether you want to stay with Kevin or not. You have a daughter who wants to find you."

"Look at it from my viewpoint, Nora. Why does she want to find me? Is it so she can tell me off or question why I gave her up? Is it so she can satisfy her own curiosity? Or does she just want to find her real father? What is it?"

"Okay, I've spoken my piece, but if I had the opportunity before me that you have, I'd at least give Kevin and his family a chance. He's a nice man, and you may be getting all upset for nothing. Maybe Jenny Johnson didn't find out as much as you think she did. Maybe all she found was your name."

Bev shook her head. "An arrest was a high price for her to pay if she only got my name. Anyway, she won't do any time, Nora. I phoned Jack Kindler about the matter. I agreed to pay all damages if he would drop the charges against her. He contacted the prosecutor, who already had a heavy caseload. They dropped the charges against her."

"You softy. I think you should stick around—at least until you know if Jenny and Kevin know who you are. If they don't, I think you should tell them. I believe Jenny Johnson wants to find her mother, someone she can identify with. Her adopted mother is gone. You're the only one left. When it comes right down to it, you have to forgive yourself, Bev, so you can move on."

Bev sensed Nora's wisdom. "I think you might be right. Besides, no matter who knows about my past, it's time to come forward."

Nora nudged her and pointed to the green van driving up the street. "You didn't do anything wrong. All you did was give birth to a child who was taken from you against your will. How could that turn anyone against you?"

Bev nodded as she watched the van. "Maybe we'll find out soon."

For the first time since Bev had known her, Katie wasn't the first one out of the van. Instead, she remained stoically poised in the back seat. However, Bev couldn't help but notice the anxious face in the front window— was it Jenny? With clammy palms, a lump in her throat, and butterflies in her stomach, Bev quelled her excitement and waited inside.

"What are they doing?" Nora stood behind her.

"I don't have the slightest idea. Maybe they're getting their courage up. I'm afraid to do anything but wait." Bev unlatched the door and crossed her arms.

The woman opened her door and stepped outside. She moved tentatively toward Bev. No doubt, it was Jenny. Bev opened the lanai door and stepped outside. In a matter of seconds, Jenny and Bev stood face to face. "Are you Bev?"

The dull, empty ache gnawing at Bev's soul had suddenly dissolved. She nodded her head and stared adoringly at Jenny. "Yes, I am."

Jenny cleared her throat and licked her lips. "Excuse me for being so forward, but I have to say that although I'm sorry for the way I went about it, I'm not sorry I found you."

"You're not?" Bev held back from embracing her daughter.

"Want another little tidbit? Your attorney's office called me a little bit ago. They told me they'd dropped all charges."

"So this is my father, huh? No wonder you fell in love with him. He was quite a handsome fellow. Did anyone ever tell him about me?" Jenny sat cross-legged on the floor in Bev's living room with the box of memories sitting between her and Katie.

"He was a handsome boy who became a drifter. I thought I loved him, but it was for the wrong reason. I wanted to get away from my father. I don't think Stephen ever knew about you." Bev shrugged. "Our situation was so weird. I'd only been linked with him a month before we married. His parents whisked him out of my life before I even knew I was pregnant. The postcard at the bottom of the pile is the only thing I have to go on, if you'd ever want to find him."

"Your parents didn't help matters any." Kevin's warmth settled her, calmed her, and made her feel supported. He'd embraced her earlier, taking his turn after Jenny and Katie. Her hope for a future with him looked promising.

"Bev, did you hate my grandpa and grandma for the way they took my mother?" asked Katie. "And would it be okay if I called you Bev instead of grandma?"

"Katie, I love how direct you are. Yes, you may call me Bev. I have to say, at the time, I didn't understand anything that was going on."

"But what did you think of them? I'd be furious. In fact, I was furious to hear how everything happened."

Jenny touched Katie on the arm and looked her in the eye. "Not now."

"It's okay, Jenny," said Bev. "I had a little anger myself after I got older, but your grandparents were aching to hold a child in their arms, Katie. I can't blame them. The situation must have seemed right to them as well. I was too young and inexperienced, and I had to go along with the plan."

"I'm sorry, Bev. That must have been tortuous," said Katie.

Bev looked up into Kevin's eyes then back to Katie. "I was young and clueless. Even so, when I look at you and see what a wonderful young woman you are, I know your grandparents gave my daughter better care than I ever could have. All is forgiven."

Jenny moved next to Bev on the sofa and took her hand. "I just want you to know I am flabbergasted about this turn of events in my life. I loved my mother, and I love my father, but I wish I could have known you as my mother. Now I have that opportunity. Is it too late?"

Bev sniffed back her tears. "Of course it isn't. You'll always be my Jane Elizabeth."

"Oh Bev, I love that name," said Katie. "Mom, that's so close to your own name."

Kevin leaned over and took Bev's other hand. "And what about me? Is it too late?"

The dark clouds had broken. With her daughter on one side and Kevin on the other, the bleak, wintry feeling she'd had the past week had disappeared. She'd never imagined the Lord would open these doors. The dull, empty ache was gone. "I give you the same answer. Of course it's not too late."

"I hear wedding bells," said Katie.

"Dad, you need to be more romantic than that. Can you at least get down on one knee?"

A flush warmed Bev's face as Kevin got down on both knees in front of her, still holding on to her hand.

"Bev, I'd like to get married—maybe at Christmas."

She gave him her best smile. "I would love a Christmas wedding, if Katie and Jenny will agree to be in it."

Bev had finally found the impossible—someone who could overlook her past and forgive what she couldn't, until now.

* * * * *

REQUEST YOUR FREE BOOKS!

2 FREE INSPIRATIONAL NOVELS
PLUS 2
FREE
MYSTERY GIFTS

Love Inspired®

YES! Please send me 2 FREE Love Inspired® novels and my 2 FREE mystery gifts (gifts are worth about $10). After receiving them, if I don't wish to receive any more books, I can return the shipping statement marked "cancel." If I don't cancel, I will receive 6 brand-new novels every month and be billed just $4.49 per book in the U.S. or $4.99 per book in Canada. That's a savings of at least 22% off the cover price. It's quite a bargain! Shipping and handling is just 50¢ per book in the U.S. and 75¢ per book in Canada.* I understand that accepting the 2 free books and gifts places me under no obligation to buy anything. I can always return a shipment and cancel at any time. Even if I never buy another book, the two free books and gifts are mine to keep forever.   105/305 IDN FVYV

Name   (PLEASE PRINT)

Address   Apt. #

City   State/Prov.   Zip/Postal Code

Signature (if under 18, a parent or guardian must sign)

Mail to the Harlequin® Reader Service:
IN U.S.A.: P.O. Box 1867, Buffalo, NY 14240-1867
IN CANADA: P.O. Box 609, Fort Erie, Ontario L2A 5X3

**Are you a subscriber to Love Inspired books
and want to receive the larger-print edition?
Call 1-800-873-8635 or visit www.ReaderService.com.**

* Terms and prices subject to change without notice. Prices do not include applicable taxes. Sales tax applicable in N.Y. Canadian residents will be charged applicable taxes. Offer not valid in Quebec. This offer is limited to one order per household. Not valid for current subscribers to Love Inspired books. All orders subject to credit approval. Credit or debit balances in a customer's account(s) may be offset by any other outstanding balance owed by or to the customer. Please allow 4 to 6 weeks for delivery. Offer available while quantities last.

Your Privacy—The Harlequin® Reader Service is committed to protecting your privacy. Our Privacy Policy is available online at www.ReaderService.com or upon request from the Harlequin Reader Service.
We make a portion of our mailing list available to reputable third parties that offer products we believe may interest you. If you prefer that we not exchange your name with third parties, or if you wish to clarify or modify your communication preferences, please visit us at www.ReaderService.com/consumerchoice or write to us at Harlequin Reader Service Preference Service, P.O. Box 9062, Buffalo, NY 14269. Include your complete name and address.

LIDIR13

REQUEST YOUR FREE BOOKS!

2 FREE RIVETING INSPIRATIONAL NOVELS PLUS 2 FREE MYSTERY GIFTS

Love Inspired
SUSPENSE

YES! Please send me 2 FREE Love Inspired® Suspense novels and my 2 FREE mystery gifts (gifts are worth about $10). After receiving them, if I don't wish to receive any more books, I can return the shipping statement marked "cancel." If I don't cancel, I will receive 4 brand-new novels every month and be billed just $4.49 per book in the U.S. or $4.99 per book in Canada. That's a savings of at least 22% off the cover price. It's quite a bargain! Shipping and handling is just 50¢ per book in the U.S. and 75¢ per book in Canada.* I understand that accepting the 2 free books and gifts places me under no obligation to buy anything. I can always return a shipment and cancel at any time. Even if I never buy another book, the two free books and gifts are mine to keep forever.

123/323 IDN FVZV

Name	(PLEASE PRINT)	
Address		Apt. #
City	State/Prov.	Zip/Postal Code

Signature (if under 18, a parent or guardian must sign)

Mail to the Harlequin® Reader Service:
IN U.S.A.: P.O. Box 1867, Buffalo, NY 14240-1867
IN CANADA: P.O. Box 609, Fort Erie, Ontario L2A 5X3

**Are you a subscriber to Love Inspired Suspense
and want to receive the larger-print edition?
Call 1-800-873-8635 or visit www.ReaderService.com.**

* Terms and prices subject to change without notice. Prices do not include applicable taxes. Sales tax applicable in N.Y. Canadian residents will be charged applicable taxes. Offer not valid in Quebec. This offer is limited to one order per household. Not valid for current subscribers to Love Inspired Suspense books. All orders subject to credit approval. Credit or debit balances in a customer's account(s) may be offset by any other outstanding balance owed by or to the customer. Please allow 4 to 6 weeks for delivery. Offer available while quantities last.

Your Privacy—The Harlequin® Reader Service is committed to protecting your privacy. Our Privacy Policy is available online at www.ReaderService.com or upon request from the Harlequin Reader Service.
We make a portion of our mailing list available to reputable third parties that offer products we believe may interest you. If you prefer that we not exchange your name with third parties, or if you wish to clarify or modify your communication preferences, please visit us at www.ReaderService.com/consumerchoice or write to us at Harlequin Reader Service Preference Service, P.O. Box 9062, Buffalo, NY 14269. Include your complete name and address.

LISDIR13

REQUEST YOUR FREE BOOKS!

2 FREE INSPIRATIONAL NOVELS
PLUS 2
FREE
MYSTERY GIFTS

Love Inspired
HISTORICAL
INSPIRATIONAL HISTORICAL ROMANCE

YES! Please send me 2 FREE Love Inspired® Historical novels and my 2 FREE mystery gifts (gifts are worth about $10). After receiving them, if I don't wish to receive any more books, I can return the shipping statement marked "cancel." If I don't cancel, I will receive 4 brand-new novels every month and be billed just $4.49 per book in the U.S. or $4.99 per book in Canada. That's a savings of at least 22% off the cover price. It's quite a bargain! Shipping and handling is just 50¢ per book in the U.S. and 75¢ per book in Canada.* I understand that accepting the 2 free books and gifts places me under no obligation to buy anything. I can always return a shipment and cancel at any time. Even if I never buy another book, the two free books and gifts are mine to keep forever.

102/302 IDN FV2V

Name	(PLEASE PRINT)	

Address		Apt. #

City	State/Prov.	Zip/Postal Code

Signature (if under 18, a parent or guardian must sign)

Mail to the Harlequin® Reader Service:
IN U.S.A.: P.O. Box 1867, Buffalo, NY 14240-1867
IN CANADA: P.O. Box 609, Fort Erie, Ontario L2A 5X3

Want to try two free books from another series?
Call 1-800-873-8635 or visit www.ReaderService.com.

* Terms and prices subject to change without notice. Prices do not include applicable taxes. Sales tax applicable in N.Y. Canadian residents will be charged applicable taxes. Offer not valid in Quebec. This offer is limited to one order per household. Not valid for current subscribers to Love Inspired Historical books. All orders subject to credit approval. Credit or debit balances in a customer's account(s) may be offset by any other outstanding balance owed by or to the customer. Please allow 4 to 6 weeks for delivery. Offer available while quantities last.

Your Privacy—The Harlequin® Reader Service is committed to protecting your privacy. Our Privacy Policy is available online at www.ReaderService.com or upon request from the Harlequin Reader Service.

We make a portion of our mailing list available to reputable third parties that offer products we believe may interest you. If you prefer that we not exchange your name with third parties, or if you wish to clarify or modify your communication preferences, please visit us at www.ReaderService.com/consumerschoice or write to us at Harlequin Reader Service Preference Service, P.O. Box 9062, Buffalo, NY 14269. Include your complete name and address.

LIHDIR13

ReaderService.com

Manage your account online!

- Review your order history
- Manage your payments
- Update your address

> *We've designed*
> *the Harlequin® Reader Service*
> *website just for you.*

Enjoy all the features!

- Reader excerpts from any series
- Respond to mailings and special monthly offers
- Discover new series available to you
- Browse the Bonus Bucks catalog
- Share your feedback

Visit us at:
ReaderService.com

HEARTSONG
PRESENTS

Look out for 4 new
Heartsong Presents books next month!

**Every month 4 inspiring faith-filled
romances will be available in stores.**

These contemporary and historical Christian
romances emphasize God's role in every
relationship and reinforce the importance of
faith, hope and love.